LISTEN

& OTHER STORIES

Also by Liam Callanan

The Cloud Atlas

All Saints

LISTEN

& OTHER STORIES

LIAM CALLANAN

FOUR WAY BOOKS

TRIBECA

To Susan,

who always does

Please direct all inquiries to:
Editorial Office
Four Way Books
POB 535, Village Station
New York, NY 10014
www.fourwaybooks.com

This is a work of fiction. Names, characters, places, events, and incidents are the products of the
author's imagination or are used in a fictitious manner. Any resemblance to locations, events, or
actual persons, living or dead, is purely coincidental.

Library of Congress Cataloging-in-Publication Data

Callanan, Liam.
[Short stories. Selections]
Listen : and other stories / by Liam Callanan.
pages ; cm
ISBN 978-1-935536-54-3 (acid-free paper)
I. Title.
PS3603.A445A6 2015
813'.6--dc23
                    2014030215

This book is manufactured in the United States of America and printed on acid-free paper.

Four Way Books is a not-for-profit literary press. We are grateful for the assistance
we receive from individual donors, public arts agencies, and private foundations.

This publication is made possible with public funds from the National Endowment for the Arts

and from the New York State Council on the Arts, a state agency.

[clmp]

We are a proud member of the Council of Literary Magazines and Presses.

Distributed by University Press of New England
One Court Street, Lebanon, NH 03766

CONTENTS

Swimmers

She drew a deep breath and tried again.

"Water offends me," Esther explained. "Rivers and lakes and oceans. I don't swim. I can't swim. I'd sooner see them all drained than risk drowning."

The young man listening—his name—his name—here it came, *Ethan*—cocked his head. Earning some sort of service hours through the parish, Ethan checked in on her each week to see what she needed— something fetched from the basement, the newspaper from the lawn, a ride to the store, a reason (she knew this) to wake, bathe, and eat.

But the newspaper had given her a new reason this week, and so she needed a new favor. They were detonating the old dam; she wanted to see. Could he take her?

He thought—it sometimes seemed to take his all—and finally said just one word: *why?*

And here she'd just said.

3

Boys. Fine. She held out a hand; he helped her up. "Because," she explained, "I used to live there, under the water."

The town of Tobin had grown up around a riverside mill at the bottom of a small valley. Then a neighboring town diverted the river to power its own mill, and Tobin withered. In summer, boggy, it became an insect paradise; in winter, a mix of snow and rain flooded basements and roads. Those who could, moved. Those who couldn't were later moved by the state when it was decided to dam the valley and flood Tobin.

But now, decades later, the dam had outlived its usefulness: it would be more expensive to repair than remove, and think of all that would be revealed when the river returned! Or so the argument went; a prime beneficiary of the restored ecosystem would be an endangered frog, tiny, the size and color of a fingernail.

Esther remembered from her childhood that it had taken weeks for the town to flood, but at the dam-clearing ceremony with Ethan, she heard them say that the valley would be empty of water by the next morning and that by as early as the week following, it would be possible to explore it by foot. Some students and professors from

Clark University—engineers, biologists, archaeologists, and, the paper reported with scornful glee, two poets—would be the first ones in.

When the speeches finished and the plunger sank, everyone waited, and Esther, hemmed in by people much taller, finally had to ask Ethan if anything had happened. She'd expected an explosion worthy of television—and the many cameramen on hand must have as well—but all she'd heard was something like a loud, quick exhale. *Pfft*, some dust, another *pfft*, then some cracks appeared, and then there was no dam. Just water pouring over the remains. It hadn't been much of a dam, two or three stories tall; Tobin hadn't been much of a town. A collection of backhoes and dump trucks rumbled to life and the crowd cheered. That was the loudest sound.

"What do you think?" Ethan asked. Esther looked away.

She would come back later to look for her sister.

That summer, sixty-eight years ago, Sam was going to teach them to swim. Esther and her twin sister, Brunhilde, who went by Bunny. There had never been much reason or chance to learn to swim before. Tobin had no pool, and you needed a car to get to one of the not-so-nearby ponds or lakes. But then the state started in on the dam, and the water rose while the townspeople watched. The mill and town common disappeared first, but that only improved the look of Tobin. The mill had been in disrepair, the common perennially scabbed bare of its grass.

When the rusty playground and the decrepit school disappeared, though, it was different. The school in particular took forever, the cornice of its broad flat roof a lingering reproach: *Why aren't you doing anything?*

But people were. They were moving as one home after another submerged. In time, just the houses up the ridge were still above water. They'd be gone, too, by the end of summer, but the families along the ridge were hanging on for just a little longer. The twins' parents had already found jobs, and a house, all the way over in Albany, but the girls, sixteen, begged to stay behind, at least until school started.

Absolutely not.

Then their parents relented: Just a week. Their new jobs were starting; they would be busy setting up the new house in Albany; the girls could give the old house, which sat just below the ridge, a final scouring search for anything left behind.

Two girls on their own in a flooding town? It might have raised eyebrows, but hardly anyone was left to take notice. And those who were noticed only the water.

Besides, Esther knew what her parents knew, which is that she did a better job managing Bunny than they did.

One week became two, and word came that the Tomlinsons, way up at the top of the valley with all their children, needed assistance, at least until Mr. Tomlinson, who'd also found work elsewhere—Boston— could find a house big enough to relocate his family. Could Bunny and Esther help?

So miracles did occur. Their horrible town became a paradise: a growing lake covered the bog and drowned its insects, the twins' parents were miles away, and the oldest of the Tomlinsons, Sam, seventeen, lived in a house the two sisters were now obligated to visit every day.

Sam. Tall as his father, kind as his mother, and a backup, sometimes primary, parent to five younger siblings. His muscles—some occasionally on view, others easily imagined—were long and smooth. But what Esther liked most about Sam was that he was still growing into whatever he would be; he wasn't done yet, hadn't hardened or set.

He didn't know that boys as handsome as he was didn't talk to Esther, or better yet, he didn't care. And so she really had believed him when, months prior, he'd told Esther they couldn't date because he was going to become a priest. Maybe he believed it, too, at least until he started dating someone else. And someone else. And someone else. And Esther stopped counting at five, and then the dam came and the math didn't matter, nor Esther's prior disappointment, not entirely. All those other girls were gone now. Their homes, too.

It was enough to make a girl smile, which Esther seldom did. It was one way to tell Esther and her sister apart. They were twins but not identical: Esther was older by two minutes, a length of time that seemed to stretch as years passed. Esther grew older and Bunny younger. Their parents had left and the twins had stayed. Esther looked out for Bunny, thought things through for Bunny—for both of them, really.

So when Sam asked if they wanted to explore the town at night by canoe, Esther said, *Of course not.* And when he replied, *Bunny, are you sure?* Esther clarified, *We never go anywhere apart.*

And Bunny, bless her, smiled.

Sam smiled back. *Never?*

He led them to where he'd stashed the canoe in the trees and explained how, night after night, he'd been drifting through the gradually vanishing streets, watching one house after another disappear floor by floor. Now, they could, too.

And the sisters did. But—together—they also watched Sam, watched him confidently thread the streets and name the stars and, some nights, sing. He had a terrible voice, but Esther didn't laugh because it seemed like he didn't know. (And Bunny didn't laugh—because it seemed like she didn't know?)

One night, he found a house flooded to its second story. He asked if they wanted to crawl in. They said no. He asked if they wanted *him* to crawl in. No.

In he went.

Esther knew he'd be fine. He was very athletic. And he was capable, responsible, especially with his younger siblings, whom most mornings he led like a line of ducklings down to wherever the water now lapped. Once, there'd been some trouble, someone had gone in too deep (Esther had heard the shouts), but there they all were at lunchtime, present and accounted for, Sam and his little brothers and sisters, every last one, smiling about their secret.

Esther listened now. For a while she heard him yodeling from room to room, but then it was silent. It was Bunny who broke the quiet—she called out "Sam!" and he reappeared a minute later, almost tumbling into the canoe.

"That's not safe." He dug deep with his paddle, pulling them away. The boat canted awkwardly and he wouldn't look at them.

"You were *scared*," said Esther, although, or because, she suddenly was. Scared of what might be happening between Bunny and Sam. It was dark, she couldn't see much, but sometimes you didn't need light to see what was going on between two people.

"Scared?" he asked. Now he turned. Now he smiled. Now he looked at Esther.

"Esther!" Bunny scolded.

"Fine," Sam said. "I was. Lot of odd noises in there, a bunch as I walked around, and the floor started feeling weird—dancy, I guess."

"What?" Esther asked.

"Like it was dancing around," Bunny elaborated, proud of Sam, perhaps of herself.

Esther looked away. *Here we go again.*

And they did go, throughout the remainder of the summer, always sticking to the rule, sticking together, until they reached the one place the rule always broke down: the Congregational church.

Every night near the end of their explorations, Sam would tie up at the church's white steeple, a job that grew easier as the water rose and the steeple narrowed. Once the canoe was secure, he stripped down to his shorts and dove in, away from the church, toward where its broad empty lawn had been. Elsewhere in town, you couldn't be sure what lay beneath. (Beneath the sisters' own clothes, though, that was certain: both wore bathing suits.)

"Jump, Bunny," he said, and she did. She always did.

"Jump, Esther," they said, and she never did.

There'd been talk about people who hadn't left their homes, and although Esther didn't believe this, when she stared into the water, she found it easy to imagine that it wasn't just her reflection staring back.

"I can't swim," Esther said, like she always said, and thought, like she always thought, that if this summer went on for twelve months instead of three, if the reservoir took years to fill and not weeks, if Bunny took a century and not what seemed mere seconds to learn to float and splash and dog-paddle and finally swim alongside Sam, there would be time and space enough for Esther, too, to learn.

"It's easy," Bunny whispered one night.

"What about breathing?" asked Esther.

"You already know how to do that," Sam said.

But Esther didn't know how to breathe, not any longer. The air was too thick. There was too much water, too much Sam, too little time.

"I thought you were twins," Sam said. "I thought what one of you did, the other could do."

"That's not true," Esther said.

And Bunny said nothing, Bunny looked at her hands in her lap, and then Esther knew.

Why Esther kept going with them—and why they let her—she didn't know. Maybe it was for safety, maybe they didn't have the heart to tell her no, maybe they were doing absolutely nothing sinister (that was one word for it) when they swam off (always together), two wet heads moving smoothly away in the dark, returning, laughing, minutes (felt like days) later. When *had* Bunny learned to swim? And why couldn't Esther? Esther, everyone knew (except Sam?), was the smarter one. They were twins, but they weren't identical.

Esther knew something was going on, but didn't know quite what. She knew Bunny had started wearing lipstick for their nighttime excursions. Or thought she knew. Esther refused to ask, and it was hard to tell in the dark, which only emphasized how silly Bunny was being.

Another example: Bunny didn't want to leave their old house, "not yet." Two blocks below the Tomlinsons, the twins' house sat on a lot that sloped back to front. So while the water was almost to the bottom step of the front porch, the kitchen door in back was high and dry. The electricity and gas were off. They ate and bathed at the Tomlinsons'; they would start sleeping there soon.

Why they weren't already Mrs. Tomlinson professed not to know. And neither did Esther. A room was waiting for them on the Tomlinsons' top floor. Mrs. Tomlinson checked its every corner each day for dust. Meanwhile, at their old house, the twins had to use candles. Bunny liked them, but candles dripped, candles attracted moths, candles did not make one look at all attractive, Esther decided as she studied herself in the bathroom mirror. Behind her, in the bedroom, Bunny slept. Esther stared. Lipstick? *Was* that Bunny's secret? There wasn't any hidden in their bedroom, not that Esther had been able to find. She opened the medicine cabinet. Nothing. She picked up a package of cotton swabs, and then a bandage tin, rusted at its base.

It was heavy, too heavy.

So Bunny had hidden it in here.

And she had. Not lipstick, but a small velveteen box and, inside that, a ring, an engagement ring, with a freckle of a diamond. Tiny, and yet the candle loved it. Moths, too, and one so startled Esther she dropped the ring into the sink, where it bounced from one side to another before it began skittering to the very lip of the wide-open drain.

"*That* was close," Sam said the next morning as they pulled away from the twins' house in his canoe. The water had been reliably rising just inches each night, but that morning, when the twins swung their feet to the floor, the carpet was damp. For a moment, Esther thought that it had rained and the roof had leaked. It had and it hadn't; the rain had poured, the roof had held, but that hadn't mattered to the water, which had climbed the stairs steadily all night. Sam claimed they'd been lucky, and Esther could only nod while Bunny gripped her small suitcase tight against her chest.

Despite its sudden rise, the water that morning was dawn-still, smooth and black. Esther asked Sam to slow the boat down. He did, and she looked back at their house, its dim outline hovering just beneath the surface like an unfinished thought. Gone was the stoop where, at six, Esther tripped and cut her forehead: *Now we can tell you apart!* her mother had said after the stitches. Gone was the front living room, so small a Christmas tree always filled half of it. Gone were the painted cabinets above the sink, and between them and the ceiling, the narrow gap where Esther, too curious, discovered that birthday presents often hid. Two cakes. Her mother always made two cakes. Esther watched the house for some time, waiting to be sad, and then, just waiting.

It didn't take long.

Mr. Tomlinson sent word: a new house had been found. He'd be home that weekend to finalize the move. The packing began in earnest now, and the Tomlinson children caromed constantly down through the house, the countless boxes, like pachinko balls. It was almost time to go.

Specifically, it was late Friday night, about eight hours before Sam's dad was due in from Boston. Esther slept fitfully. Her bed at the Tomlinsons' was more comfortable, but the house was more noisy. Water had muffled so much before. Here, children coughed or padded to the bathroom. Stairs creaked. The screen door flapped once in the wind, gently. And then twice. And then Esther opened her eyes, looked across to see if Bunny was having trouble sleeping, too, and saw that she was gone. Esther got to the window just in time to see Bunny's white form running up the road, alone.

Esther dressed, and tried to find a silent path down the stairs. An impossible task, and yet no one roused, so accustomed were they to the old house's constant creaking and settling at night. Or, Esther thought, to Sam's constant coming and going at night, bound for the priesthood. And so Esther went straight to where he'd told her about his supposedly divine calling: the park, the picnic shelter, which was also the place where he had kissed her—Esther—that one and only time. She knew his landmarks.

"It's just—it's just a ring, sweets," Sam was saying as Esther arrived out of the shadows.

Esther tried to work her face into one of concern or confusion but was only halfway there when Bunny cried and flew into her arms.

"We were going to get married," Bunny sobbed. "We *are* going to get married. But—we were leaving tonight. Because his father—and— Esther, he—" Bunny pulled away to explain: "Sam gave me a ring, but now—now I've lost it."

"You're—what?" Esther asked. Showing surprise was unexpectedly easy, perhaps because she was surprised. They really were here. And so was she.

"You can't leave," Esther said, to Sam. "We're not done packing the house. Your father's not home. Our parents are in Albany." All irrelevant reasons, and she seemed to have a limitless supply. "The water hasn't reached your house yet. The reservoir's not full. We'll be seniors in the fall. Homecoming is in October. It's okay if your date's from another school. Another state." Esther wasn't crying. "We're only sixteen." Bunny stared at her. Esther stared at Sam. She'd delivered this speech to the back of his head; he was staring at the water. Esther said one last thing: "You—were going to teach me how to swim."

Sam turned now. To Bunny. "Are you sure? Because with the water rising, we had to get out of there so fast. Are you sure you took it when you left your parents' house? I told you—I told you to leave it be, not to take it out all the time."

"I didn't!" Bunny cried. "Ask Esther!" He didn't. Esther didn't move. "I mean, I did," Bunny said. "I didn't much—but sometimes—but I always put it back. Always. And I know I took the box with me that morning."

"You're sure?" Sam asked.

"I know, because I thought, I should check it, but I couldn't—Esther was right there."

Neither Bunny nor Sam would look at her.

"Now," Esther said, "I'm here." At some point, Sam would have to talk to her. Tonight, tomorrow, in Boston, in Albany. Inside a church.

Outside. Someday.

"I'm—I'm so sorry, Esther," Bunny said. "I shouldn't have—it was just that—I know—I've never—I *wanted* to tell you, so much. And show you the ring. But I couldn't—he—we—agreed that, just until—"

"I don't remember you carrying around anything like a ring—" Esther said.

"Oh, of course you don't, I was afraid you'd—and I—I—well, I'm certain, I'm certain I—" Bunny looked at Sam, the water, even, finally, Esther. "I looked everywhere today, Sam. Everywhere. It's not at your house; it's not in the yard. I even checked the kids' rooms—I think it's still—it's back at our old house!"

"We'll just—just get another one," Sam said. Esther studied him. That tiny ring. It had cost him everything. "Not right away, no, but another one."

"Sam," Esther said. She could feel her heart breaking for him, but when he looked up, she felt something else, something like nothing.

Sam looked down again at his watch, and then back down the road toward the flooded town.

"The water's high," Esther said as Sam paddled, not sure if she was being mean or if she was terrified. Chimneys, antennas, decabled telephone poles teetered here and there like the last guests in a darkened ballroom.

Bunny stared into the black water, as though she'd be able to spot the ring amid the reflected stars and shards of moon.

"At least your home was near the top of its street," Sam said. "The water can't be as deep."

"No, no, it can't be," Bunny said. "And I kept it in the medicine cabinet"—Esther invisibly avoided a glance from Bunny—"in a tin, on the second floor, and there was a window right there. A Band-Aid tin. I don't remember if I left—I think I did, I think I did leave the window open!" She turned to Esther. "It's so silly, but I remember thinking, 'Oh, the water's going to come in all over the floor and make a mess, and won't that be a bother.'"

"Hush now, Bunny," Sam whispered, so tenderly that Esther shivered. Then Esther saw the shortwave antenna that had been atop the neighbor's house.

"That's it, next door," Esther said and gripped Bunny's hand because she couldn't not.

They floated closer. Sam poked his paddle down and found the roof. "That's good. The water's not too high, not yet." He had Bunny tell him again where the ring was, and then stood and began to undress. Even in the moonlight, they could see the goose bumps rise across his skin. He started to undo his pants, but stopped. "I, uh—oh, I'll just be a second." He paddled to the neighbor's antenna and tied a triple knot. "No drifting," he mock-scolded. He had a crooked tooth, just the one, only apparent if he smiled at you, or if you kissed him back.

They all studied the water. It was scarier at night, but it was also better at night. During the daytime, you saw things. Oily slicks. Discordant colors, orange, electric green and blue. The occasional turtle. Once, Esther was certain, a snake. And toys—worst of all were the dolls.

At night, though, you could see almost nothing. "I'm just going to swim back over there," Sam said, "dive down, into the window, open the cabinet, then—back here."

"It's so dark," Esther said, still uncertain how she was going to stop this.

Sam spoke quickly. "We've got the moonlight. And if the cabinet is close to the window, maybe I can just reach in."

"You can!" Bunny said. "The bathroom wasn't big. The medicine cabinet was right there."

Sam carefully left the boat. "Okay," he said. He turned and swam over to the submerged house. He found the roof with his feet and waved back at them, still grinning. Then he slid beneath the water.

"Sam!" Esther screamed, but it was too late.

He popped up a moment later, sputtering. "Wrong window!" he shouted. Down again. A longer minute this time, and he splashed back to the surface. "I can't reach it from outside. But the window's open! I'm going to swim inside."

"Don't!" Bunny cried. "Be careful!"

Esther felt sick; what happened when he didn't find the ring? What if something worse happened? "Watch out!" she yelled, but he was already underwater. A longer minute this time, followed by another one, followed by nothing.

Bunny screamed, on and on. Esther held her sister with all her strength and tried to keep the canoe from rocking. *Give up, give up,* Esther kept willing Sam, but she knew he wouldn't, and a small part of her hoped he wouldn't, because that was another reason why Esther loved him. Sam was right, better than right, even when he was wrong.

"Untie the rope!" Bunny shouted. "Untie it! Untie it!" She crawled away from Esther and attacked Sam's knot, but it wouldn't give. "Esther!" Bunny cried. "Help me! Please, *please.*"

It wasn't until Esther fiddled with the knot that the knowledge came to her—what was happening, what had happened. Bunny was in the opposite end of the canoe, keening for Sam. Esther finally got a loop loose, and when she did, she thought, *Wait till I tell Sam I beat his knot!* and then wept as she realized she'd never be able to tell him. Frantic, Bunny finished the knot for her.

Bunny paddled with her hands and Esther with the paddle, but once they'd reached the spot, they could only stare. There were no bubbles, no debris, nothing at all. Just the moon, those stars. They waited another moment, another, and Bunny said, "It hasn't been that long"—and it hadn't, not in human time, maybe fifteen minutes, but forever underwater.

"Bunny!" Esther hissed or shouted or shrieked, she wasn't sure, only that the voice sounded nothing like hers. She was furious. With

Sam, with Bunny, with herself. If Esther had learned to swim, *she'd* be over the side now. Why wasn't Bunny? "Go!" Esther shouted.

Bunny put two hands on the gunwale. "Esther, I—"

"Save him!"

"Esther," Bunny said. "It's—it's too late."

"You can *swim*," Esther said. "He taught you how to *swim*. I would go, but I can't swim. Bunny, get in the water, get in now. Swim to him. Brunhilde!"

"I'm not good enough! You saw, you know. I could only swim when he was—when I was with him!"

"*Teach me how,*" Esther said. Again, the other voice. Who said the things Esther said? Who did what she did? "Teach me how to swim. I'll save him."

"Esther." Bunny's voice was thin; she was hardly breathing. "It's too late. And you can't—you can't just learn to swim, just like that."

"You—did."

And so they fought, punching and kicking and pulling, the canoe rocking, but never tipping. Bunny stopped Esther from throwing herself into the water, once, twice, and then settled her down, only to catch her a final time. At that point, the twins collapsed into the boat and drifted, smothered between the ever-rising lake and the softening sky.

Sam's father found them late that morning. He was riding in the back of a police launch. While Bunny cried whatever tears she had left, Esther told him what had happened. That Sam was just goofing around, just trying to show off. They had tried to stop him, but he wouldn't be stopped. Esther said nothing about Bunny. Nothing about the ring. Nothing about how Esther loved Sam more. Esther thought Mr. Tomlinson took it well, his face devastated but resigned, until he looked up at Esther, then Bunny, then them both, and said, "My son died because of you."

And the way his words burrowed into Esther's head, lodged in her mind, tiny and sharp and painful, she thought for a second that the ring itself had wormed its way in there, and would burn behind her eyes forever.

But it wouldn't, it couldn't; the ring was in Esther's pocket.

The dam had not been large, but the area exposed seemed vast, far bigger than the reservoir. Certainly it took longer than expected to make the old town navigable. Esther read that on one of the university's first forays, an eager undergraduate striding ahead found himself sinking in mud that acted like quicksand, and another emerged with tetanus. Decades of settling silt meant firm ground was much farther beneath the lakebed than initially estimated. The scientists declared that heavy equipment would be required to make access safe. Others argued for nature to take its course—hadn't that been what this was all about?

Esther didn't know, only that it was now late fall, and that evaporation, cold weather, and, finally, a lot of shoveling had reportedly made the place somewhat accessible. She called Ethan. They made a date; he even called it that.

He did not bring flowers but a wheelchair. She didn't use such a thing, hadn't asked for one, but here it was, and she found it handy. Getting out of the car, looking up the path into the old town, she'd been wobblier than she thought. And he seemed to like pushing. As before, as ever: boys.

The old brick school was still intact; it looked no worse than it ever had, and maybe even better. Like everything else, it was roped off.

A sign explained that this might be a future visitors' center. The town common, now a field of muck, housed a row of nervous-looking boxed and burlapped trees awaiting spring.

The Congregational church was a sight, just like the photo in the paper. The steeple had not collapsed, though the structure supporting it had. As a result, the steeple had fallen straight down into the sanctuary, and only the very top now peeked out over the roofline.

Some streets had been cleared down to the original pavement; in other places, new pavement had been poured. Farther in, wooden walkways were laid, and past that, as the town began to climb the hill, the wood gave way to dirt. Esther's wheelchair couldn't manage it, nor did she want it to.

She rose and walked, Ethan alongside. He talked until she told him not to. Almost there.

And then—there was the neighbor's place, there was the man's shortwave antenna, there was nothing else. A cleared concrete path, the twins' old front walk, led up to where their house had been. Ethan, talking again, explained that many homes had collapsed when the water withdrew, and their wreckage had been cleared away.

"Was this your place?" he asked.

She walked to the end of the concrete and looked.

Long, delicate strands of bright green grass crowded inside her home's old foundation.

Back when the dam still stood, when where she was now standing was still at least two stories underwater, she had thought about taking the ring and putting it back in its place. But Esther didn't know where the ring was and hadn't for years. The day after Sam disappeared, the ring disappeared.

Her twin sister, too.

And soon enough, the Tomlinsons. But Bunny—

Bunny—

Bunny knew how to swim.

Had she swum to Boston, Esther often wondered? Or New York? Los Angeles? Bunny on a bus Esther never saw her take, in Bunny's fist the ring Esther never saw her take back.

Or had Bunny swum back to the house, their old house? Through the cold and dark, deep and then deeper, searching for Sam, finding him waiting, floating, eyes, mouth, arms, open?

He had waited for her, and she for him. Esther waited now, and soon she felt the water—icy and quiet as the old truth—around her toes, her ankles, her shins, her knees, higher.

The Bear Hunter

EDDIE HAD FOUGHT HARD. AT LEAST FOR A LITTLE WHILE, AT LEAST AS long as he thought it was just some of the other guys messing with his tent, trying to poke and punch him through the thin nylon shell. He was the new boy; he could have expected this, especially because he had a hoard of candy that he wasn't sharing. But now the hoard was gone. The bear had eaten some, scattered the rest, and wandered off, as if bored by all the blood, which fascinated me. I know that's a strange word to use, *fascinated*, but I was, I am, at how empty and motionless that boy was. I don't mean Eddie. I mean the kid next to him. I mean me.

Art, on the other hand, couldn't stop moving. Art was my friend, at least at the time. (After we got back, we hung out less and less, and I couldn't even say now when was the last time I saw him.) Art and I had been left in charge of Eddie. And, in a way, in charge of Mr. Mulroney, who was something like an assistant scoutmaster that summer. Dr. Paber told us Mr. Mulroney would be an excellent scoutmaster someday, but I wasn't so sure. Back then, I wasn't so sure what made Dr. Paber a doctor, either, since he was a history teacher. But Mr. Mulroney: first of all, he was pretty young to be called "Mr.," plus he smoked, plus he didn't know much about scouting. He did know a lot about the military: he had been in the army, in fact, but said he had broken a leg during basic training and had to quit. He still had a lot of the gear, including some guns, which he and Dr. Paber disagreed about, sometimes loudly enough that we could hear.

See? Mr. Mulroney had said, and we all knew what he meant, though, of course, we couldn't really see anything after the bear left— flashlights and headlamps stabbing about, the fire smoking, the moon fighting the trees. Anyway, what Mr. Mulroney meant was, if he had been allowed to bring his guns, the bear would be dead. Instead, Eddie was, or almost. Dr. Paber said we had no way of knowing something like this would happen. Something this terrible could only be a surprise.

Which was a crock. I mean, I wasn't surprised. I had my own reasons, of course, given what had happened at home earlier that year, but I bet all the scouts on that trip half expected something terrible and bloody would occur. It's hard to explain, other than to say that whenever we went camping, we somehow fell into this easy, ongoing, matter-of-fact, almost casual relationship with death. We saw dead animals all the time. We killed things (small things, insects) all the time. We went to the Sierras several times a year. A dozen or so boys, two adults, no cell phones, through relatively untraveled national forests. It wasn't that long ago. Or it was. What I mean is, there was no net. I think if you'd asked us, we would have given even odds that someone would die at some point in our scouting careers. It would have struck us as *likely*. But we were too dumb to be afraid. And we'd trained as scouts, which I guess is another way of saying the same thing. And, of course, thousands of people, scouts or otherwise, went hiking every year, and still do, without trouble.

But what about the one time something did happen? What were you supposed to do? Use the handbook?

Early on, I'd figured out that the handbook pretty much only talked about situations you could handle. The really bad stuff—getting the top of your head taken off by a bear, dying—that stuff they didn't have in there. But you knew it happened. In another troop in town, a boy had died. Of cancer. Before that, I didn't even know kids got cancer. The handbook never went into things like that. The handbook had stuff like, if a scout gets seriously injured, build a litter from branches and tarps and carry him on out of there.

But that night, it was dark and everyone was scared and the branches weren't long and straight like in the book and the tarp started to slip and Eddie to slide and we were ten miles and one seven-thousand-foot pass from the trailhead, and Dr. Paber finally muttered, "Fuck it, we're going for help." He told Art and me to stay with Eddie, and Mr. Mulroney, too.

Dr. Paber rounded up the rest of the scouts and off they went, flashlights slicing everywhere until he yelled "Save your batteries!" and they disappeared.

Eddie was so pale. He'd been pale since the day he'd joined the troop, not a month before, and it was something we all noticed, of course. Eddie was quiet, too, didn't say much other than to say where he was from, Minneapolis, and that he'd just about completed the requirements for his Star badge. His mom had brought him to the first meeting, and she was pale, too, and so was the baby she was carrying. But this pale tonight was a new pale. I bent to look closely—and here again, I blame scouting, which made almost every interaction an opportunity for decoding *(study this badge, this leaf, this bird, this insignia, this sky, this salute, and determine, what does it* mean?)—and I wound up sitting down heavily.

Which is how *I* briefly became something to study and solve: Mr. Mulroney asked if I was okay and Art said I was in shock and Mr. Mulroney said to shut up. So Art did, we all did, until Art mumbled something like "We need to elevate his feet," which was straight out of the handbook, and Mr. Mulroney said, "All the blood will pour out his head." He told Art to check the book. Art said he was talking about me, not Eddie. Mr. Mulroney said he didn't give a rat's ass about me.

And so Art checked the book. This seems crazy to me now, that with a kid right there lying on the ground, bleeding out after a bear attack, one of us would stop to check the *Boy Scout Handbook*— that we'd even have conversations, for that matter, that our mouths could form words and our minds thoughts. We should have been hiding or crying, breathing too fast or not at all. But we weren't. I can't explain it, although I keep trying to. I mean, more than anyone, I should have been upset. But I wasn't upset. I was so damn curious.

It's not enough of a word.

Neither was *pale,* but it was all I could think to say—"He's so pale"—to Mr. Mulroney, who was standing now, facing away from us, looking down the trail.

"He's lost a lot of blood, Jeremy," Art said before Mr. Mulroney could answer me.

Mr. Mulroney exhaled and gave Art this long look. After the litter debacle, Mr. Mulroney had cradled Eddie's head in his lap, and I saw now that his pants were still covered with Eddie's blood. The light was bad, and so all I could think—again, this is wrong—was that someone had dropped a big, frosted chocolate cake in his lap. "Look at the moon, Jeremy," Mr. Mulroney ordered. I looked up; Art did, too, which kind of ticked me off. "Full moon tonight," Mr. Mulroney went on. "It's lighting him up, making him pale." Mr. Mulroney finished this bit with a good solid stare at me, and I nodded. When Art finally caught my eye, I could see that he was frowning. Mr. Mulroney poked a tiny stick in the fire for a while, and when he pulled it out, the tip was molten orange. He found a cigarette and held the stick to it, puffing. It took a while for anything to happen, and I looked back to Eddie.

I tried passing my hand over Eddie's face. "He ain't going to see that," Art said, which made Mr. Mulroney get angry—or organized. He assigned Art to "sentry duty," telling him to walk the perimeter of the campsite, around and around, so we'd have some warning if another bear came. And Mr. Mulroney told me that if I really wanted to help, I could stop waving my hand over Eddie's face and instead hold up his head. The jackets we'd balled up weren't working.

I eased myself right alongside Eddie. Mr. Mulroney carefully arranged a towel (mine, full-sized, which Art had teased me for bringing) on my lap and carefully laid Eddie's head there. All of this seemed to happen without sound, without air. I could feel Art looking at me, at us, looking so hard it felt like he was pushing us, but I couldn't hear anything, not until Mr. Mulroney straightened up and said, "There."

I studied Eddie. Again, the bleeding had stopped. Initially, some had wanted to put the piece of scalp back on—one of the guys had found it, puked, and afterward carried it like a strip of bacon over to where Eddie lay—but Dr. Paber shook his head and didn't move. I guess if it hadn't been clear to us before that Dr. Paber wasn't a doctor-doctor, it was at that point. Mr. Mulroney simply said it was too dirty to stick back on, and told us to wrap it in a wet neckerchief. Eddie's head, meanwhile, we just kept wrapped in more neckerchiefs. That was kind of the scariest thing, watching those neckerchiefs turn red, one after another, almost instantly. It was eerie the way the red just seeped through them; it spread so quickly, like one of those nature movies that speeds up all of a sudden: it's a bud, it's a flower. Watching all that, a couple other guys had gotten sick, and Dr. Paber had Art turn his flashlight off. We'd use the moon, Dr. Paber explained, even though there wasn't much to use the moon for. The blood seemed to be satisfied with the neckerchiefs.

Eddie's lips were pursed now, like he was going to speak. He'd screamed when it happened, first like he was scared somebody was breaking into his tent—which the bear was—and then—it must have been when the bear started scraping away, looking for scents—Eddie screamed this weird, really high, really freaky scream, like I'd never heard, except maybe in movies, or the day this guy broke his arm during gym. I didn't get over there in time that day, but I heard you could see the bone sticking out. The way that scream echoed around the gym—in a way, we could all see the bone.

Eddie and I were supposed to be tentmates. I mean, Art and I were tentmates originally, but Art got in trouble with his folks, and all of a sudden he wasn't going on the trip, and that meant I was going to have to buddy up with Eddie. Standing orders were that I wasn't allowed to sleep alone. But then Art did whatever it was he had to do, and he was back on the trip, and we were back in a tent together, and Eddie was on his own.

I looked over at Eddie's tent, which was crumpled in a heap, like somebody had popped it with a pin. But the bear had done a lot worse than that. He'd gone right through the rain fly, right through the tent roof, and bam, he was in, and on top of Eddie. I think I was still sleeping. The first thing I had heard was Mr. Mulroney shouting, "Knock it off!" Then I heard Dr. Paber a few seconds later say, "Shit, Mulroney," and then I heard whistles blowing, and then Art and I were out of our tent, watching the bear shamble off, and listening to that scream.

But Eddie hadn't made a sound since. He was lying really still, but I knew he wasn't dead. Not that I was an expert, but of all the guys in the troop—and maybe this included Mulroney and Paber—I was the only one who'd actually ever seen someone (not an animal) dead, up close. The trip, in fact, was part of a whole summer designed to make me forget all that. I put my hand on Eddie's arm, and it did feel cold, but of course, it was a cold night out. I leaned a little closer, and just as I heard Mr. Mulroney say, "Everything all right there, Jeremy?" some tiny scoop of air, a breath, kind of smeared across my cheek. So I'd been right. He was alive. I told Mr. Mulroney everything was fine. In a lot of ways it wasn't, but for now, it was okay. Sitting there, even with Eddie doing nothing, I was getting to know him, in a way.

We sat like that for some time. Every so often, I'd let my hand linger above Eddie's lips, just to see if any air was sneaking out, to make sure he hadn't died yet. The rest of the time I spent looking around. It was an incredible night with that moon. It was so bright it took away a lot of stars, but in return, you got to see just about everything you could want to see: the trees, the meadow, the mountains beyond. It was like somebody's backyard lit up for a party. I didn't like how the moon made some things even darker, though: around the edges of the meadow, under the trees, in the moon's shade, was this deeper black, the kind of haunted-night dark that just swallows people up who step into it. Art was avoiding those dark places, too. Mr. Mulroney fed the fire.

After settling Eddie on my lap, he'd seemed unable to come close to us.

That was fine. And I didn't want to talk either, but Mr. Mulroney kept staring at us, and I felt like I needed to say something. I had a lot of things I could have said, of course, but I didn't want to. I'd moved to LA, joined the troop halfway through the school year. I'd been the new kid before Eddie. And so I'd learned: what you do first is deflect.

I said to Mr. Mulroney, "His mom's going to be really upset."

"Yours, too," he replied and then launched into a minispeech that I tried to ignore. *Life wasn't fair* was the gist, I guess. That here I, he, Eddie, Art, all of us, had just come up to the Sierras for some fresh air and open skies and trouble-free days, and trouble had found us. And he was sorry. Sorry for us, and sorry for himself. Maybe even sorry for the bear. The bear didn't know what he was getting into, getting into that tent.

"Mr. Mulroney!" Art shouted before I could say anything, not that I was going to.

Mr. Mulroney didn't turn around, but just tilted his head back and shouted up at the sky, "What?"

"I need to go to the bathroom," Art said quietly, coming closer.

"Hell, Art," Mr. Mulroney said. "You've never asked me before."

"Well, I didn't want to, you know, abandon my patrol."

"Piss away, scout," Mr. Mulroney called. He paused. "Just don't—just go where I can hear you." Art looked at him. "Don't wander off, is what I'm saying," Mr. Mulroney said. "Who knows where the thing is now, okay?" Art left, and Mr. Mulroney turned to me. "Where were we?"

"I don't know," I said.

"Listen," Mr. Mulroney began. He stopped and shook his head. "It's not that—"

"I'm right here, Mr. Mulroney!" Art shouted, but he sounded far away.

"Good, Art!" Mr. Mulroney shouted, but not loud enough, and they had to exchange shouts again.

I looked down at Eddie. His color seemed to be improving, although when I looked up to check the moon, I realized it was setting. Maybe it was the color of the sky that was improving—it was getting closer to dawn.

"Here's the thing," Mr. Mulroney said. "They've got you kids running from one 'No' to another, when in fact, what's really going to kill you is—"

He stopped and looked at me, and for a split second, I thought, *Oh, someone's told him about me.* But I studied his eyes, heard him speak, and realized, *No, he doesn't know anything at all.*

"I don't think Eddie did drugs, did he?" Mr. Mulroney asked. "Didn't smoke?" I didn't know; I shook my head. "I'm sure he didn't," Mr. Mulroney said. "But: it didn't matter. He got mugged by a bear."

I waited, but Mr. Mulroney seemed settled on this. I was trying to figure out something to say when an incredible new scream pierced the night. My first thought was Eddie, though he wasn't moving when I looked down; my next thought was Art, and in a second, he was running toward us, mouth wide open—but it was bizarre; the sound wasn't coming from him. Anyway, it was a girl's scream, a woman's scream, really. It wasn't a scream any of us could make.

"What—what was that?" Art asked.

Mr. Mulroney looked a little shaken himself, but instead of answering, he came and knelt by Eddie. He ran a gentle hand across the neckerchiefs that wrapped Eddie's forehead, asked Art to get some water to resoak the scalp neckerchief thing, and finally put his ear to Eddie's mouth and looked straight down his chest, just like they told us to do in CPR class.

"Hey, boy," Mr. Mulroney said quietly. The scream came again. Mr. Mulroney rocked back onto his heels and settled into a squat.

"Mr. Mulroney," Art said. He hadn't gone to get the water.

Mr. Mulroney nodded. "There was this guy in the barracks, early on in basic, who always said you should never scream. When you scream a little bit of your—what did he call it? Your—I can't remember. A bit of your soul escapes was what he was saying." He stood up, looked around. "Now that scream, that was a mountain lion, I'd say."

"It sounded like a girl!" Art said.

"They do," Mr. Mulroney said. "Read it in a magazine."

"But it could be—"

"It could be a girl," Mr. Mulroney said. "We've not seen anyone else during our three days on the trail, though, and we do know there are mountain lions around here. I vote for the lion."

I asked if lions were attracted to blood.

"They're pretty shy, if that's what you're asking," said Mr. Mulroney. It wasn't what I was asking. "We'd be lucky to see one."

"Lucky?" Art asked.

"XYZ, scout," Mr. Mulroney said. Art looked confused for a moment, and then figured it out and zipped up his fly.

We didn't hear the lion scream again. But Art didn't go back out on patrol. He and Mr. Mulroney took seats by the fire, and eventually Art slumped over and fell asleep. Mr. Mulroney just stared into the fire, and I studied Eddie. After a long time of turning things over, I'd decided that the mountain lion's scream we'd heard might be Eddie's soul escaping. I liked Mr. Mulroney's friend's theory, and this seemed the best way to make some sense out of what was happening. A mountain lion? A bear? A kid missing a hunk of his scalp?

I shifted a bit and a little moan came out of Eddie. It wasn't his soul. It was the opposite; that sound meant Eddie was alive. Mr. Mulroney came over. Art blinked awake.

"Eddie?" Mr. Mulroney stared at him. "Eddie, buddy? Eddie?

C'mon boy, what do you got in there? Give me something here." Eddie lay silent, and after a minute, Mr. Mulroney had to check his breathing again. Eddie was so still. I started holding my breath.

"Something's coming!" Art shouted.

Mr. Mulroney froze, and for the first time, I was scared.

This *was* just like what had happened to my family.

There had been no tent, no bear, no moon, none of this, but otherwise, it was exactly the same: When you needed help most, that was when you discovered there were some things you couldn't help. Sometimes things happened that you couldn't stop.

"How's he doing?" asked Dr. Paber, emerging from the dark. He and the rest of the troop had either made good time, or they'd given up.

"Hey, Doc," Mr. Mulroney said. "He's okay. I mean, considering."

Dr. Paber knelt and looked at Eddie, and then at me. "You okay?" he asked. I nodded. "It's going to be all right," he said. I shook my head, because it wasn't going to be, not ever again, but he didn't know that, no one did, and I'd long ago given up making people understand. He exhaled and stood and cleared his throat.

There was a cabin just over the pass. There was a man inside.

He lived there during the summer, was a kind of park volunteer. He did odd jobs around the park, including an unusual one that interested Dr. Paber most.

"He's coming to get the bear," Dr. Paber announced.

"No way," Art said.

"What's he know about first aid?" Mr. Mulroney said. "What about a chopper? Rangers? The friggin' air force?"

Dr. Paber shook his head. Apparently the man didn't have a radio, just a giant flagpole. If there was trouble, he ran up a red flag, which could be spotted down at the ranger station some twenty miles off. When they saw it, they sent help.

"That's a hell of a goddamn system," Mr. Mulroney said. "This is the twentieth century. Buck Rogers and all that. No radio? Kids today should be able to go hiking, go to school, for that matter, and not get killed. Not get shot."

"No one's getting shot here, Mulroney," Dr. Paber said slowly, and came back over to Eddie.

"Sounds like the bear is," said Mr. Mulroney.

"Good riddance," said Dr. Paber.

I had to ask. "He's really going to hunt down the bear, Mr.— Dr. Paber?"

"That's right, he's going to kill the bear before he gets help for Eddie," Mr. Mulroney answered.

"*Enough*," said Dr. Paber, but Mr. Mulroney just shook his head and wandered off into the meadow, where he stood looking up at the pass.

"The man was telling us that this is standard procedure," Dr. Paber said. "After one of these encounters, especially one where the bear draws some blood—they track the bear down and capture him. Well, shoot him. Once they've lost their natural fear of humans, they're not safe."

"The handbook says bears are vegetarians," said Art.

Dr. Paber looked after Mr. Mulroney. "And that they're curious. And like candy. Listen. The book's only a book." Dr. Paber finally turned to Art. "But I wish Eddie had read it."

I knew the bear was close by. Really close by. There's no saying why I knew this, but I did, and anyway, it turned out to be true.

The bear hunter arrived about forty-five minutes later, just as the night was making that change that you never notice unless you're sleeping outside. It was still pretty dark, but there was enough light coming in at the edges of the sky that you could tell morning was coming and nothing was going to stop it. It sounds like an obvious thing, but already on that trip I'd realized that some nights, if you weren't sleeping, if you were just lying there, awake and listening to all those sounds, as I always was, and had been for months—all those branches cracking somewhere out there, sometimes closer, sometimes farther—that moment of morning sometimes took forever coming.

The bear hunter had a horse and two dogs. That much I had already kind of imagined—except for the second dog, I guess, and definitely not the hunter's outfit. He was wearing this raincoat sort of thing and a baseball hat with a long bill. I couldn't see what was printed on the cap, but it seemed disrespectful. I mean, Eddie was here dying, a bear was about to get it, and this guy shows up in a ball cap.

Mr. Mulroney raised both hands like he was either blessing the bear hunter or getting held up. I saw the bear hunter shake his head no, and Mr. Mulroney moved away and found Dr. Paber. They got into some sort of discussion, and the bear hunter leaned out of the saddle and yelled something to the dogs, which bounded into the forest. I thought he'd gallop after them, but he didn't. Instead, he looked over toward the campsite—toward Eddie and me. I couldn't quite tell if he saw us, but he started the horse walking our way. Mr. Mulroney and Dr. Paber looked up at him, and he came to a stop, and got off. Dr. Paber and the bear hunter came over, leaving Mr. Mulroney holding the reins like they were the string of a balloon.

The bear hunter knelt and looked at me, at Eddie. "Don't know much about first aid beyond what you done," he said, twisting toward Dr. Paber. Then the man turned to me: "You okay?"

People had been asking me this for months.

"He's going to make it," the bear hunter declared, looking back down at Eddie. I wanted him—the bear hunter—to die, right there. What did he know? What did Dr. Paber know? I looked over at Mr. Mulroney, and he was just standing there, staring.

I looked at Eddie. The coming daylight was doing a lot of things, and one of the scariest was how it made Eddie less ghostly, more real. The light didn't exactly make things clearer, but closer. His face, his head, seemed huge now.

Dr. Paber told all the boys to stay really close to camp, and told me that if I wanted to get some rest, I could. I'd done a fine job with Eddie; I was going to grow up to be a doctor someday.

I wondered if he thought that's why I'd been sitting there. It wasn't.

I'd been sitting there because it was the most incredible thing I'd ever seen, Eddie's body hanging on like this, trying to figure out whether or not to go on living or keep on dying.

I hadn't noticed right away, but while everyone had been out in the field, Eddie had started breathing in this new, funny, way, like he was scared—these little, short, rabbit breaths: huh-huh-huh-huh. I checked for his pulse, but I couldn't find it. I checked for my pulse and I couldn't find it either. We'd learned how to find a pulse during first aid. We'd even practiced, but that never went well; we usually just ended up wrestling or choking each other. Anyway, Eddie calmed down a little, his breathing began to slow, and so did mine.

I heard the dogs again, really close this time, and suddenly, racing across the meadow, faster than anything I've ever seen run, came this bear.

I was amazed how small it was. It was big enough, but it wasn't huge. It wasn't much bigger than one of us. The dogs were right after the bear, too. The rest of the troop was yelling, starting to run, and Mr. Mulroney was in a crouch, his arms spread wide, like he was going to hold everybody back or like he was going to scoop the bear up. Dr. Paber was behind him, pulling at the back of Mr. Mulroney's shirt and shouting.

But the bear ran right past the two of them, and the dogs followed, one passing in front of Mr. Mulroney and Dr. Paber, and one behind. At the edge of the meadow, the bear started to run into the trees, stopped, turned around like he'd forgotten something, and started scrabbling up this ponderosa pine. The handbook said the bark smells like vanilla and it's true. The dogs skidded to a stop beneath, howling now, and the bear clawed away frantically, climbing and slipping, scrape, scrape, scrape. Something about it made me feel I couldn't watch, but when I looked down at Eddie, it was worse. All I could hear was the scraping, those claws, and all I could see was that scalp.

The bear hunter gave a short whistle, and the dogs backed off, just like that. He threw them something out of his saddlebag, and they went after whatever it was, completely forgetting the bear, who was now on this branch, maybe twenty feet up. You'd never have thought when he'd started that he would get that far.

The hunter got off his horse, slapped it on the side and made some sound, a cluck that sounded for all the world like his tongue was made of wood. The horse trotted into the meadow and started in on the grass. I saw Mr. Mulroney look after the horse and smile, and I felt a little better, too. It was just the bear hunter and the bear now, and the bear hunter wasn't doing anything other than standing there, beneath the tree, hands on his hips, looking up. We'd just hold the bear at bay until the rangers came with a net or something.

The bear hunter fished for something in his pocket, and turned his cap around backward like a catcher. And then, from a place I couldn't see, he brought out a pistol. A pistol! You didn't have to be into guns to be surprised by this. A man goes after a bear with nothing but a pistol? Where was the big shotgun? This was the wrong way to end things. I looked for Mr. Mulroney to see if I was right, and sure enough, he was staring at his feet, shaking his head. Even Dr. Paber was looking away, pretending to watch the horse.

I checked Eddie, but he was still sleeping—I'd come to think of it as that. A shot rang out. I looked up. The bear scuffled in the tree, but didn't fall. Once he'd found his perch again, he let out a yowl. It was more of a scream, really, deeper and scratchier than the mountain lion we'd heard, but a scream, no question; no one would say it wasn't. The bear hunter shook his head, and looked at his gun. I looked at Eddie. His eyes, long closed, were now open and colorless, if that's possible. He looked at me for a long moment, and another, and suddenly, I thought that he had died, right then. I couldn't decide if I had missed it or seen it, and I was angrier than ever at the bear hunter, and at Dr. Paber, at Art, at all of them. Not at the bear. And I didn't think Eddie was angry at the bear, either. I rested my fingers gently on his lips and waited and waited. I thought about doing CPR, but imagined Mr. Mulroney telling me not to.

Another shot. I didn't look up this time. It was too noisy; it was too light. I looked down at Eddie, and he lay there, just staring at me, which was wrong. He needed sleep. I swept my hand down his face, across his eyes, just like on TV when they want to close the victim's eyelids, and sure enough, it worked. I slowly began to unwrap his head. The bleeding had stopped, and the neckerchiefs stuck to one another, but one by one, they came undone, until it was just Eddie's head again, the bright red gash much darker now and, for some reason, smaller. I reached over for the damp packet we'd preserved the scalp in, and unwrapped that, too. I picked it up carefully by a bit of hair, and tried to lay it back into place. I checked Eddie's face, but he took no notice. I started placing the neckerchiefs back on him again, but they wouldn't wrap as tightly.

A third shot, followed by crashing branches. Some shouts. I still didn't look up. I could see it well enough. I could see it, all of it, and I didn't want to see it. I didn't want the morning to come, the rangers to come, the moon to leave, or the bear to die. I didn't want the bear hunter and his horse and his dogs and his baseball hat, his joke of a gun, and his silly flagpole. I didn't want to know for certain that Dr. Paber wasn't a real doctor. I didn't want to know what had really happened to Mr. Mulroney in basic training or why he was hanging out with a scout troop. I didn't want Art to tell me what had happened, again and again and again. I didn't want to remember I'd ever wanted Eddie to die and that I'd wanted to watch.

But suddenly I heard Eddie cough—just like that, a little cough, the same little cough the dying person makes in movies and you know they're going to be all right. He blinked open his eyes again and looked at me, not saying anything just yet, but I knew he'd be talking soon. And he'd be fine.

I didn't hate him. I had every right to, the therapist said. I'm talking about my brother now, although I guess I could be talking about Eddie, too, and for the opposite reason. My brother had died, and Eddie had lived. Eddie had pinked into life like he was taking a cue from the skies. The color came up from inside him, life surfacing beneath my hands as though I'd done this with my hands, though I knew it didn't work like that, because it hadn't with my brother. I was the one who found him, and I was too small and he was too big, I couldn't get him down, and so I found a stool—this sounds so stupid, but I can only tell you what I did—I climbed up to him and held his head and tried to blow into his mouth, like in the book, smack his chest, ignore the rope. I was too late.

I had wanted to see Eddie die because part of me still wanted everyone to die, because it wasn't fair. But I also wanted to see it because

I wanted to *see* it, that moment, so I could know what it looked like, so that when I'd finished building the time machine I was dreaming of, when I'd learned whatever was necessary, I could go back, right before, and stop my brother, stop it from happening.

I never built the time machine. I never went on another hike with those scouts. And I'd like to say I never think about that trip whenever I lie down at night, but that's not true. It's not the bear that haunts me, though, not Eddie, not that missing piece of his head. It's the bear hunter, deliberate and sure, always coming. And it's that body, heavier in death the way bodies are, falling. I can feel it. I can hear it. I can see everything, despite the dark.

BEDTIME STORY

HE WAS THE FIRST LOVER SHE'D HAD WHO HAD A SECRET DEEPER, and sillier, than hers: he was totally, utterly, wickedly afraid of the dark.

Oh, but whom was she kidding? Bridget was twenty-four, and he was the first lover she'd had, period. That was her secret.

Bridget had gone on *dates*, of course. She'd gone to an all-girls Catholic high school, Mary Star of the Sea. Dating was unavoidable. The old joke—that the school's acronym was SOS, meaning *save us*, meaning *get me out of here*—never failed to raise a smile among certain outsiders, noninitiates, non-Catholics, but always fell flat with the girls. *Keep us in* was what the girls mostly thought, *enough with these mixers.* Sophomore year, Bridget was on the swim team, in for a season of surprises: She was fast. The goggles really hurt. She felt more naked with the slick, taut Lycra racing suit on than off. And one sunny Saturday, flip-turn flags fluttering and the stands full, there was her coach saying: *We arranged this coed meet just for you. Come on now, go talk to them.*

*You can do it. Be brave! Just one word, that's all it takes. Just go up to them, just say—*Hi.

It took her seven years, but she did. Thanks not to her coach, but someone with an even worse approach to aquatics management, the lifeguard at her local public pool in Baltimore. The pool was inside a long-shuttered high school that had been converted to a community center. Then a jail. And finally, a municipal warehouse, but through it all, the pool remained. Occasionally, the lifeguard did not. Sometimes he monitored things from the chair, sometimes from the deck, sometimes from the windowless guard's office, and sometimes, apparently, from the sidewalk outside while he walked home, unaware or uninterested that he'd just turned out the lights on his last two swimmers.

Save yourself.

But she could, because she had learned at Mary Star of the Sea that what a girl needed most in life was not a boy but books, and anything else could be had merely by pulling yourself up and striding toward your goal. In this case, that was the half-lit exit sign at the far end of the room, and she would have made it, too, had she not heard the high-pitched cry from the deep end. Someone was scared. Not Bridget, so she went to help, and there he was. Not just anyone, but that guy, cute, who'd been showing up lately, didn't stare at her, once lectured the guard about leaving. Now he needed her assistance. This she provided, and he, in turn, provided coffee, and then dinner, and then he called his au pair *(I can't stand her, but when I call late like this, she doesn't complain, so I guess I can't)*, and then he and Bridget decamped to another spot for dessert, and then a bar for a nightcap, and then another bar where they mostly just kissed.

He was divorced—"catnip to a Catholic girl, right?" he joked, but she ignored or forgave him, mostly because he said it so despondently.

And because he was named Laurel.

"Like the wreath?" she said, and she saw it happen; she saw him start to reply to what he'd thought she'd say, only to rewind and listen again.

"Everyone always says, 'Like Laurel and Hardy?'" he said in a hush, like she'd discovered a new element. Obscurium.

"He was the brains of the act," Bridget replied and saw she'd now delivered the second part of the one-two punch. Thank God for SOS and its senior-year electives—and its sophomore requirements, like classics.

And for lonely, divorced quasi academics who were suckers for smart girls.

"He *was*," Laurel blurted. "No one knows that! Hardy *golfed* on his off-days. Laurel went back to the set and futzed with the script, the lighting . . ."

But Bridget had gotten only an A– in The Legacy of Silent Film, had taken the class during the dizziness of senior spring, and so she panicked now: *Laurel* was the actor's last name; what was his first? Larry? Fritz? Couldn't she just get credit for things she did know? The names of the first five books of the Bible. The guy Homer called Tamer of Horses. The twenty-three Helping Verbs. That had been freshman year, the year of memorization, stuff she'd remember for life.

Is am are was were be being been has have had do does did shall will should would may might must can could.

But what *did* you *do* with those words? Meanwhile, this Laurel was saying something—she saw his lips moving, and they were pretty, and she kissed him, to shut him up, to get things moving. She was twenty-four. SOS!

Stan—

The silent actor's name dropped onto her tongue like a bright, sweet butterscotch, and for a moment, she couldn't stop herself, she was opening her mouth, she was going to tell him this, too, but he misread her, thought she was just adjusting, getting really serious about this kissing thing. And, she thought, maybe she was.

A few months after, Laurel invited Bridget to move in with him and his two children, Thomas (seven, and his name Laurel's choice) and Jasmine (four, her name the only thing the deserting wife had left behind). The au pair had quit, so there was a room open.

Stan Laurel had a way of showing you that he was in on the joke by acting as though he wasn't. It was almost a tell. Bridget's Laurel was harder, and easier, to read. The open face, the worried eyes. This was a joke, moving in, had to be, he wasn't serious.

She needn't worry about "living in sin," Laurel said next. And: if she *was* worried, she could pretend she was the new au pair—would that make it better? He'd tell the kids that anyway. For a while.

So it was a joke, and not. She said no. He begged. She said she'd be happy to help with the kids—they were sweet—but for money. He could continue dating her for free, though. (Her tell was a simple one. When she joked, she smiled.)

He said if she needed money, he had another job for her, a real one that would put her grad degree to work.

Her degree. Another joke, not intentional. She did not have one, but rather half of two.

She'd fled to Baltimore from postcollege life in Los Angeles, to attempt a graduate degree in creative writing. But she'd quickly abandoned that for a master's program in social work—same subject matter, less filter, or so it seemed. But now she was on the verge of abandoning that, too, even though she'd been the only student to pass, on the first try, her legendary professor's legendary pop quiz: a midnight phone call threatening suicide. The professor was very good at playing the role. Bloodshot eyes: among Bridget's classmates, *that* was the tell, that they'd been awoken late, been rattled, been unable to return to sleep. Bridget slept well, before and after the call. She wasn't afraid of the dark. But of her classmates? Yes, a little. Now they were always calling her.

But Laurel was calling on her for something else, a chance to reenter the writing world, from the other side of the classroom. Laurel ran the continuing education program of a local college, mounting dozens of classes month after month, everything from macramé to memoir. In a pinch, Laurel asked Bridget to cover a fiction workshop. "Not so different from nannying?" Laurel said.

But it was: Some weeks went better than others, though every week got her talking with people who were interested in writing. Interested in publication, too, but unlike her former creative writing classmates, Bridget's students were most concerned with the words, the way they went down on the paper. They struggled. Bridget liked that they struggled. It was hard work.

Some of her students made it harder. It startled her, time and again, how many students used the class as group therapy. Some realized this; some didn't. But most wrote out of pain, or wrote *to* pain, the words, sentences winding down the page until they found the place, again and again, where it hurt most. This man had abandoned a friend at a critical time. This boy had tried drugs for the first time and found them "simply astounding" and marveled, with increasing despair, how each subsequent high wasn't as "sticky green great" as the first one.

For the most part, though, Bridget could still workshop the stories as stories, not case histories, and whenever students tried to draw her out on the topic—*Haven't you done this, Bridget, written things out to figure things out?*—she nodded: she had, but she'd not always shared that writing. She talked about public versus private, which, listening to herself, *did* sound very thoughtful, professional, but which was also, upon later reflection, completely hypocritical.

And what about your kids? What do they think?

Recently, Bridget had tentatively—ridiculously—called Laurel's children "her" kids in the classroom, in vague, oblique little anecdotes she told so as to better bond with the other working parents and because, well, it felt *normal* to talk about one's kids, and Bridget wanted to try that, practice for the life they'd told her at Mary Star of the Sea was due her, one with a mate, a family, a quiet, private life out of harm's way. After college, before Baltimore, she'd worried how life would work out and was now half-comforted to see simply that it *could* work out.

Messily, but happily. Ever after. Right? Los Angeles hadn't worked, grad school hadn't worked, not even after two tries, but Laurel—somehow this had worked, was working. Somewhat.

Her saying no to moving in had helped. Her saying yes to teaching had helped. Her saying yes to watching the kids a few afternoons a week, her depositing only the first check and then letting the rest pile up uncashed, her spending the odd night all night and, eventually, many nights: that had helped, too. Helped both of them, or so she thought.

But the awkwardness grew. The kids were sweet, but they weren't her kids. Laurel was sweet, but he wasn't her husband. And he was good at some things but bad at others, like humor, like still being scared of the dark.

Worse, the dark was starting to scare her, too. Not intrinsically but circumstantially: afraid to make a sound, wake a soul, she would creep from her room to his in the dark, or vice versa, to lie together, always both back to where they were supposed to be come morning. Once Jasmine had come looking for Bridget in the spare room and yelped when she discovered her gone. Laurel had shot up but Bridget put him back down, palm to sternum, and flew down the hallway. *I was just in the bathroom*, Bridget said. *I had a bad dream*, Jasmine said. *I have those, too*, Bridget answered, and then stepped on a Lego—searing pain—and screamed and everyone awoke and gathered and reassured and yawned and smiled and in the morning it was a funny story.

Maybe life *was* like a silent film, the occasional stumbles only cause for comedy, the train never reaching the damsel draped across the tracks, the lovers finally embracing, the camera irising in on the kiss, tighter and tighter, until it was just their heads, their lips, until the image was gone, everything black.

Everything.

A newcomer joined Bridget's course midway through, announcing loudly that he had seen it all, he'd been in prison, he didn't scare. They should sit up and pay attention to what he wrote because they weren't going to read anything like it anywhere else.

He didn't say what he'd been in for—maybe, Bridget thought, for stealing Christmas presents, because he looked a bit like a Santa, albeit one who'd lost too much weight, and thereupon his job. But he wrote dark, bitter, misogynistic stories, and when he asked Bridget if she would show what he'd written to her agent, she answered no, not even stalling like she usually did. Because she didn't have an agent. Because the writing was bad. And because an ex-con had lived a hard enough life that he could take bad news straight up, right? He didn't scare.

He sent his answer, a scrawled note, right to the house, like he was following the script of some nonsilent movie, or, worse, the script of his own story. Or maybe it wasn't a note, maybe it was a story. It was called "Hangman," the victim's name had seven letters, the murderer was the victim's creative writing student.

Bridget hid all this from the children—the wide-eyed lying awake, the rage, the worry. How this one man, or how everything, including not being able to work out at the pool in months (classes, Laurel's kids, Laurel), had winnowed her, made her forget. She couldn't hide it from Laurel, though, who insisted she call the police. University protocol. And she should sleep at Laurel's every night from now on. "Also protocol?" she asked, and smiled, but it wasn't funny. Nor was the plainclothes policeman who arrived while Bridget was home alone with the kids, trying to get dinner ready, attempting to go a whole sixty-minute stretch without ducking into the closest bathroom to stare at the mirror to see who was there: Bridget the swimmer, the savior, the prize midnight pupil—or the one with the bloodshot eyes?

She told the kids the man was going to ask her questions because he was a newspaper reporter, and sent them to watch PBS. Which was good, because the policeman asked about terrifying things, and Bridget didn't like it when he left. Not because of anything he said, but because as he turned to walk out the door, she realized that underneath his shirt was a bulletproof vest.

Santa was arrested—the "story" he'd sent Bridget prompted an interview with his parole officer, which went badly enough that the officer wound up in the hospital and Santa in custody. In his story, the victim got seven chances to get the letters right, but in his life, he faced a justice system that allowed for only three strikes. Santa was hustled off to prison, where he'd write the rest of his life.

Bridget kept all this from Thomas and Jasmine. Skillfully, she felt.

Laurel announced that he was proud of her, too.

And while it wasn't that Bridget didn't believe Laurel—his pride in her, it was one of the things she liked most about Laurel, other than the way he'd looked, or felt, in his swimsuit that first night—Bridget did feel the air change, the way the fiery Santa Anas back in California signaled their coming madness with a single hot puff pulsing out of the desert.

But maybe what was pushing her off-kilter was the coming discussion they'd promised themselves, and the children, about the truth, about Bridget, about her moving in because she loved Laurel and he her and both of them *both of you, Thomas and Jasmine.*

But the kids wanted to talk about the reporter. Especially scary-smart Thomas, he of the X-ray vision, the one who could see everything, even or especially things he did not understand—who, Bridget assumed, already knew about her and Laurel—Thomas wanted to know why the reporter had come.

Laurel broke in: "Because Bridget's a *writer.*" Laurel had been furious that Bridget had let *his* children see a policeman in their house: *Lest your fears become theirs.*

But her fear was the old fear, which is that if you fell for a boy and it was the wrong boy, you might keep falling, never knowing when you'd collide with whatever was coming, only that you would, and that it would hurt, like a Lego in a hallway, like a pool deck in the dark, like a train on the tracks, like Hardy, the old silent-film star, stroke-silenced the last year of his life, like Laurel too ill to attend Hardy's funeral. Stan Laurel was a writer and wrote for eight long years after Hardy died, but refused to go on-screen ever again, not without his friend.

"Have you written a book?" Thomas asked.

Bridget shook her head.

"You should!" Thomas said.

Laurel told Thomas no. Or maybe he was telling Bridget no.

The four-year-old, Jasmine, loved color. Fall leaves. Pizza with all the toppings. Candy aisles and circuses. She asked, "What color will it be?"

"Blue!" said Thomas.

"Red!" said Jasmine, who insisted on reading one Christmas book a night, no matter the time of year.

Bridget thought, but did not say, *I'm tired of red, of blood, of threats, of students always committing suicide in their stories, or killing off pets, grandmothers, bad guys, good guys. Wrong guys. Of anyone's stories where anyone dies. I'm tired of everyone everywhere always dying at the end. In the dark.*

But mostly, Bridget thought, *I'm tired of red.*

Jasmine wasn't. Bridget tried to brighten up: "Let's do the title first." Bridget checked to see how Laurel was taking this. Not well.

"You should call it *Spaghetti,*" Jasmine insisted. Made sense. It was going to be a red book. And Bridget had made spaghetti tonight because that didn't require a knife, and thus, if Santa burst in, there would be less weaponry at hand. But wait: should she have kept a knife handy for self-defense? Plot, setting, arsenals: she'd have known better if she were a real writer. Or a real mom.

Red.

And so she was scared. Of Santa, of Laurel, herself. She'd let herself fall. Not for a man, but a notion. For the idea that what she wanted right now, wanted most, was kids and cookies and carpools, staying up late, staying over every night, reading the kids to sleep, and only the sweetest of books, so they would dream, like Bridget—and, she'd thought, like Laurel—only the sweetest of dreams.

Thomas said, "You should call it *Angels in the Darkness.*"

And that was her cue to cry. Because, looking at Laurel, she saw what he thought. That she'd failed as a mother before she even got a decent crack at being a mother. She'd gone and screwed it up big time, blowing that one crucial test of parenting, which was sucking it up, whatever it was, and not letting the kids see you fall apart.

She watched Laurel start to fall apart.

We are their world, he'd once told her, both universe and the universe's protective outer shell, and as a parent, you apparently had only one job, which was to make sure the glass didn't crack, that the sun always shone, that it never got dark.

But it did. It was dark now: *Angels in the Darkness*. Bridget saw Thomas's angels instantly, these tormenting winged creatures, like angry, makeupped, heavy-metal hair band rockers, black and bloody and altogether evil. Later, while Laurel tucked them into bed, Bridget would look on and know that this was what the children thought of: dark angels. And that they thought of them because Bridget had introduced this darkness into the house.

Some mother she would make, Bridget.

And she would. But that night, it was Jasmine who said, "Don't cry," and Bridget didn't.

"I'm not crying," Bridget said. She looked at Laurel.

Laurel turned away from the kids, looked at Bridget, and he didn't have to say *go* because she was already going, already gone.

But Thomas spoke first. "Angels in the darkness are the angels who sit with you, in the dark, when you are scared."

Bridget tried to nod her head, not look at Laurel.

Thomas went on: "They don't do anything else but sit there. But that makes you feel better, doesn't it?" He looked at Laurel, at Bridget, and finally, at Jasmine.

Jasmine nodded her head, once: *Yup.*

"Some people are scared of the dark," Thomas said and looked at his dad.

Bridget looked at Thomas, then Jasmine. Not Laurel. Bridget didn't mean to say what she said next, but she wasn't in a position to police herself—not that she ever had been, apparently. Not that policing herself would have ever been right.

Bridget said, "What about when it's light?"

Jasmine said, "Maybe there are light angels?"

Thomas said, "No, there aren't."

And Jasmine, who usually fought with him, said nothing.

And Laurel, who usually scolded Thomas for needlessly freaking Jasmine out, said nothing.

And Thomas got up, went to the wall, and turned out the light.

Light from the other rooms bled in. Jasmine got up to cut the switches off. Thomas ran around, racing her, it was a game, but neither Laurel nor Bridget could stop them until everything was dark, until the only light left was the deepening dusk outside, the digital green of the appliance clocks, and a general glow that seemed to hang in the air like smoke.

Grown-ups and kids huddled in the hallway outside the bedroom. It wasn't so dark they couldn't see each other. But it was dark. Bridget could hear that Laurel's breathing was shallow, and she could hear him try to hide that fact. What she needed to do now was open her arms wide and draw them—Laurel, Thomas, Jasmine—all of them in, hold them close before or until the angels got there. But she couldn't. Her skin was wet, she was naked again but for that Lycra suit, which, after all this time, was still worse than wearing nothing at all.

Outside, a car door slammed. Footsteps followed.

The man who'd threatened Bridget had died: the police thought she should know.

But what nobody knew then was this, that years later she would be married to someone else, a kind, gentle boy who was scared of nothing *other than losing you;* that they would be living in Newport Beach, California, where three of her four children spent summers as junior lifeguards; that when Bridget listened to the house settle at night, she sometimes thought of Laurel and Thomas and Jasmine that dark evening in Baltimore before the police knocked.

"See?" Thomas said. "Don't you feel better?"

"Shh," said Laurel.

"Don't you see them?" whispered Jasmine.

"Shh," said Bridget, and it became an exhale, and at its extent, she found herself smiling, her lips parting, about to offer up what became, over time, her shortest, simplest, favorite prayer, the word her children

found her with when they couldn't sleep, the word she offered her husband when they were the first to awake on a sleepy Sunday, the word she greeted herself with whenever a painful memory came swimming back, that single word that ever since always dispelled the dark. *Hi.*

And as the calm and quiet gathered, she might close her eyes once more.

When the Lights Go Down

Rita Loomis had fallen asleep at her own retirement party.

Her colleague Amelia Monroe noticed this from the back of the room, embarrassed for Rita, and grateful for herself. Because until that moment, Amelia was sure *she* had been the most embarrassing aspect of the program. After all, as principal, Amelia had hired Rita thirty years ago. And here Rita was departing first? Rita, who'd looked not much older than her sophomores that first year? Granted, Rita was retiring young, at just fifty-five, but people could do the math if they cared to: *If Rita is retiring, what's Amelia Monroe still doing here? Goodness, she must be 107 by now, or close to—*

Amelia was not. She was sixty-one. An active, alert sixty-one. Active enough, for example, that were the impossible to occur—that Amelia would retire, that she would allow a party to be held in her honor—she would most definitely not fall asleep, not during the requisite slide show, not during the cutting of the sheet cake, not during the presentation of the certificate and frame that they'd spend less than a latte on.

Amelia favored a particular spot during mass gatherings in the auditorium (always standing, always back left, near the fire doors). She was on the verge, however, of going forward to nudge Rita awake. But it turned out that Bob Meinert, biology, would get that honor. He was sitting next to Rita. And so when Rita really lost it—let herself slump onto Bob's shoulder—Amelia hung back and watched as a series of questions materialized and dimmed in her head, just like the slides Rita was now missing:

Why hadn't Rita ever married?

Why didn't I ever marry?

Did Rita ever have a thing for Bob?

Wait, is Rita—

She was. Dead. Because it turned out that even with a master's degree in biology and twelve years' experience teaching the subject, Mr. Meinert could no more rescue Rita Loomis from a massive stroke than could the paramedics who soon arrived.

These things happen.

Amelia brought up the lights. She locked open the fire doors. She made a path for the gurney. She felt like everyone was watching her, but they weren't. They were watching Rita leave. Behind them, at the front of the auditorium, the slides continued to bloom and fade on-screen until Amelia finally went forward and turned them off.

I don't want to die.

She could, of course, just write that on the questionnaire, since it was true: "What are your goals?" the sheet asked.

But Amelia didn't want to startle anyone at the shiny, antiseptic new fitness center. She'd watched the facility go up not a mile from school, passing it every day on her way to work. True, she had daily scoffed at the notion that anyone, most of all she, would go there. For one thing, her townhouse complex had a gym. Free. She'd never been inside the place, but she'd seen the picture on the brochures, and back when she'd served on the owners' association, it seemed like they were always approving this or that expenditure for the facility. Someone used it.

Yet here Amelia now was, about to make her own expenditure and join this completely superfluous gym. But that was the only way, she'd read in a magazine at the doctor's office (another post-Rita errand): *If you pay for a gym, you'll go to the gym.* Besides, the first month was free.

But gyms had changed. It wasn't just barbells and those odd machines that seemed to place a dozen pulleys and gears between you and the weight—they had all that business at the high school. (When she'd asked him to recommend a gym, Mr. Burbush, the phys ed teacher, had offered her the use of the school's weight room, which only confirmed her opinion of him: truly dense.) This new gym was like a dance club. Not just the music—and she'd have to see to that straightaway, get the volume turned down and the selection changed—but the lights, the mirrors, the colors. Television and computer screens everywhere, and on sale in a cooler by the exit, a bizarre, tropical-aquarium-worthy spectrum of bottled and canned drinks.

Maybe she would look into her townhouse complex's gym after all. It was certainly convenient.

"No cheating!" came a voice from behind her, and she turned around, flustered that she'd made so little headway on the questionnaire. The saleswoman had asked her to fill it out while she went and fetched a "personal trainer" for an introductory tour.

"Ms. Monroe," the boy addressed her, although he wasn't a boy, of course, not now. He was a responsible adult, had a job—personal trainer—and a name: Tim Prado. Tim had graduated a couple years ago. Amelia had an excellent memory, never forgot a name.

"Mr. Prado! How's college? Are you on break?"

"Graduated." He smiled. "About ten years back, I'd say."

Was she still capable of blushing? That is, did she color, Amelia wondered? She knew what blushing felt like, of course. She just was no longer sure what she looked like when she did. But Tim made no sign of noticing; he just kept smiling. Ten years out of school—out of *college*—and looking well, she thought. She'd never have pegged him for this life—he seemed to be the promised "trainer"—but she'd learned that one could never tell. Tim had begged her for extra funds for the spring musical. At least she thought that's how she remembered him.

"I saw you looking around there, Ms. Monroe," Tim said, "and I thought, that's just like me, that time I was taking a test outside your office. And you saw me looking around and thought I was cheating."

"Were you?" *Oh, Tim*, she thought. *You may think you have the drop on me, but you don't, none of you ever did or do.* She smiled, but stopped when she saw Tim involuntarily flinch.

83

"No," he said. "I mean, I wish I had. I got a bad grade if I remember."

"Well," Ms. Monroe replied, having learned long ago how to apply ice after the sting, "I certainly don't."

And then Tim Prado blushed.

Amelia went ahead and signed up for a full year. Membership plus six months of personal training services. How could she not? In addition to the free month, they happened to be having a 50-percent-off special that very day. It wouldn't have made sense to not join, and what was the purpose of going to this fancy gym if she didn't try some of the fancier things? If young Tim Prado could show her how to, say, climb onto, or into, that standing eggbeater thing or whatever it was and stay balanced, that would be lovely.

Tim had told her that she didn't really need to finish that initial questionnaire, but she'd told him straight out that her goal at the gym was improving her health. And then he'd asked how old she was—quite impertinent of him, she'd thought, but he'd waited for an answer, not looking the least ashamed, and she'd finally figured out that he had some professional reason to need to know this, that it would affect how he shaped her fitness regimen.

Fifty, she'd finally told him, finding it fun, even necessary to joke. And when he said, *Wow,* she said, *Fifty-seven,* and when he said, quite earnestly, *You look fabulous for fifty-seven,* she hadn't really been able to say anything at all in reply. She couldn't really remember if he'd been a handsome boy—he was handsome enough now—because she never really noticed that, not about any of them. There were so many years of so many students, and other than names, the most information she could ever really store about each was "good" or "bad." Tim had been good.

So it was strange, really, that he wasn't wearing a wedding ring. Perhaps he was gay? Which was fine. For him. She knew people had wondered as much of her: all those years, unmarried. But she wasn't gay. She was hard to please, is what she was. It made her an excellent principal and a lousy date. There had been two or three men over the years who had interested her in a specific sort of way, and there had been Frank, a shipmate from the first and last cruise she'd ever go on, but in general, the problem with men her age is that they wanted more of a pet than a partner. Someone to tend to, a bit of warmth next to them on the couch while they watched TV.

Frank, yes, still sent the occasional card. He'd not cared about her being so headstrong, not cared so much as all the others anyway, but that was apparently because alcohol softened everything for him. (Everything.) Nevertheless, he was a charming man, enjoyed a slow dance. That's how he got his exercise.

Tim made her buy new sneakers. A ridiculous expense. The soles on the ones she had were hardly worn, even after however many years it had been. But Tim seemed serious, and so she followed his advice, bought the sneakers. And the stretchy clothes. And even, on occasion, the drinks. There was one in particular he recommended, and she acquiesced; it didn't look quite as ghastly as the other bottles in the cooler. Truth be told, it did give her a little pep. At $1.95, she wasn't going to spring for one every day, but it was nice to see it glowing there in the cooler each day as she left. A treat, ready when she wanted one.

Tim, too. She'd remembered so little about him from his school days, and she now marveled at this. How could this one have escaped imprinting upon her memory? He was kind, thoughtful, assertive when appropriate. Always complimentary, and not falsely so. Just last week, he'd mentioned that she was acquiring good tone, and even though it had taken her a bit too long to figure out what he'd meant—surely he wasn't talking about her humming? her tan? her hair?—she'd accepted his kind words gladly. If she were thirty years younger, she'd be trying to figure out a way to get him to ask her on a date.

Good thing she wasn't, because he figured it out all on his own. She wasn't even quite sure if it was a date, in fact. But here she was, seated in the grass in the park, listening to a summer concert with Tim Prado beside her. And some of his friends, too. Luckily, none of them were former students. And if they wondered at her tagging along, they thoughtfully breathed not a whit about it, not even allowing their faces to silently betray what must have been their utter mystification.

But she was the truly mystified one. After the concert, there was that reading by that author that he'd thought she'd like (she'd not, but that was beside the point). There was that annual festival in the historic quarter that she'd never managed to get herself to, at least not until someone had asked her along. There were the dinners out. Movies. A play. All of it quite normal, and apparently normal was a big goal for Tim these days.

Tim had had an unpleasantly busy life since leaving high school. He'd gotten a girl pregnant the summer after graduation, had married her, had joined the army to get money for college, had lost the wife and child to another man, had left the army, had started one school, then another, had tried New York and then Los Angeles. Had found exercise was his salvation. Had found his way back to his hometown. Had found all his old friends were gone.

And then, had found his former principal walking into his gym one day. *Imagine that,* he suggested, and she'd tried to. She'd tried to imagine how it all ran together, how it could possibly be true that, after thirty-nine years in education, after thirty years as principal, after handing Tim his diploma some fourteen years ago, she could find herself sitting not two miles from her house in a restaurant she'd never tried (never would have tried), at a table for two with a man she'd never, ever, have asked out on a date. It was a date.

In the end, the problem wasn't that the waiter—actually more than one—asked, or suggested, or insinuated, that she was Tim's mother.

It wasn't the evenings out with his friends when she finally was able to detect some indecent curiosity, or confusion, behind their otherwise blank faces and smiles. It wasn't Amelia's friends, either, not the ones in town—indeed, she'd not quite mustered the courage to introduce him around—nor her real friends, out-of-towners, flinty folks she'd met at conferences over the years. That's where their self-adopted nickname came from, flintsters, because that's what they were, flinty women who were never, or were no longer, married.

Amelia never used the term *flintsters* herself; she wasn't quite sure why Myra and Janice, who'd coined it, felt the need to separate themselves off like some rare and failing species.

"He's just a gold digger," said Myra. Janice murmured assent. They met for monthly conference calls.

"Whatever the county or TIAA-CREF has in store for me," Amelia said, "I doubt it's enough to attract him. He could do better."

"He wants a mother," Janice said.

"Is he an orphan?" Myra said.

"Doesn't matter," Janice said. "That's what they start with; it's what they all want to end with, men: a mother."

"He could do better there, too," Amelia answered and looked at the clock to see how long it would be before they hung up. And she sat back and let them do the rest of the talking, because, for all of her gym-going, her toning, her smiling, her laughing, her holding hands, and—my Lord, it had been perfectly wonderful, hadn't it?—kissing (and more, everything, but she was not, would never be, the type who talked of such), she had to sit down, catch her breath.

Because she'd finally figured out that thing, that thing that had been bothering her all along, that little dark rivulet that ran through her every conversation with Tim, their every date. Especially every movie.

And now that she'd figured it out, she'd have to cancel her gym membership, hug Tim tight, kiss him extra close, one final time.

It was Rita Loomis. Rita hadn't been sixty-one when she'd died. Not even fifty-seven. But death had lurked for her all the same, had come and snatched her after the lights went low and the slides of her life began. She'd had a massive stroke; she'd slumped onto Bob Meinert, who, Amelia learned, *had* loved her from afar, had daydreamed of her head lying on his shoulder, just so, in the dark. And she'd died on him.

We grow up, we graduate, we retire. Old and young, we die.

It had always been this way, Amelia knew, and that had always been just fine with her. Students might cry and complain, but the facts were facts, and the more facts you knew, the more likely you were to get an A.

But now Amelia knew this new fact, that she was in love with a former student, with Tim Prado, who was kind and handsome, who'd stumbled in his life but now stood and had somehow found it in his heart to court her, woo her, make her heart pump like she'd never known it could.

And knowing that—well, that made dying impossible. Unbearable. And yet, here was Rita insisting she would. Amelia could go to the gym every day for five hours, for ten. Amelia could eat right and live right and kiss great, and she'd still find herself in an auditorium one day, sitting beside her Tim, holding hands in the dark as the music began, as the photos of her life swelled on screen and her death drew near.

Except it didn't. She didn't die, just like Tim hadn't left and locked the door behind him when she'd told him her real age, sixty-one. All he'd said was *Really?* And *You amaze me every day.* Or something like that. They were walking out of the gym at the time. Tim started to set up a date for the weekend.

"Tim," Amelia interrupted. "You don't understand. That's old. I mean, this—this is old."

"I wasn't the best math student, it's true."

"I'm serious," she said.

"About what?"

And then, finally, Amelia Monroe surprised herself. She'd never mastered the eggbeater exercise machine, she'd never gone and bought another of those weird fluorescent drinks, but she did do this, this one startling act: she spoke.

"Serious about you," she said.

Rapturous young love, rock climbing, fathering and mothering a family—that sort of thing would be left to other, longer—and altogether ordinary—lifetimes.

For Tim, for Amelia, for them both, there would be the gym, there would be dinner, there would be the still-electric pleasure of holding hands and discovering how nicely they fit.

But for tonight, there would just be this improbable retirement party, Amelia's very own, complete with interminable slide show. The organizers had asked—actually asked—if it would be okay to include a shot or two of Amelia with Rita, in younger days.

Of course Amelia had agreed. And she'd liked the result. She'd liked Rita; she'd liked the photo they'd found, both of them smiling real smiles, a photo Amelia knew and had occasionally wondered about, because she could never remember what was, at that moment, bringing the two of them joy.

But now, with Rita smiling on screen and Tim smiling beside her, Amelia knew. Here she was, Amelia, and there she was, Rita, and between them now, this moment—who knew how long it would last and who cared?—found the two women together, aglow, alive.

Mr. Fantastic

Fat Frank wouldn't take off his pants. Never mind that the studio was freezing; it was Melody's last day. Everybody was doing it: Clean Joe Green, weekend sports anchor, he was doing it. Even Melody, pulling a solo weekend anchor slot on this, her last day, she was doing it. And she *never* did this sort of thing. But she wanted to—wanted everyone to—tonight.

Frank continued his stately progress to his place on the set. Trademark girth, trademark limp, trademark Fat Frank.

"C'mon Fat Frank," called Joe, who was wearing a yellow tie, blue blazer and red boxers with bright white polka dots. He was shooting Nerf hoops with a few fully clothed crew members. Frank took his seat and began looking over his script, pen at the ready. At least Joe wasn't hassling him to "shoot a few." Almost all forms of athleticism, even Nerf athleticism, seemed designed to embarrass Frank.

Four minutes to air, buzzed a voice over their earpieces, or IFBs.

"Fat Frank," Melody pouted. "My last day."

Frank's pen skipped, just a bit. *Your last day,* he had written last night: the first draft of his note to her. It was awful; it rhymed. The seventh draft was in his pocket. It was hardly better, but it did not rhyme.

Frank smiled. Melody went to her place. The station's "arts critic"—his contract mandated the title—Frank usually taped his segment in advance, but had made an exception for tonight, for Melody. His script was short, and what notes he'd added consisted mainly of a dark-blue *M* that he'd been embroidering in the margin with his ballpoint. He looked up, made eye contact with Joe, but not Melody. Then back to his script, underlining the last word of his last line, his tagline for going on fifteen years: "*Fan*tastic." Around town, his nickname was "Fantastic Frank." Around the station, it was shortened to "Fat Frank," which he was—just twenty pounds shy, in fact, of three hundred (a threshold also limited by contract).

"The camera adds pounds," he used to tell people, when he could still joke about it. "And they accumulate."

Mariners scored again, Joe, came a voice over the IFBs. Joe missed his shot.

"What's the big deal, Frank?" Joe took his place behind the desk. "Oldest prank in broadcasting. Nobody sees, so nobody knows. Jack Palance used to do it."

Frank stared. "You mean Jack Paar?"

"Jack Frost. Jack Diddily. When the best-looking thing on two legs"—he nodded at Melody, who was following the exchange absently—"at this station tells me to take off my pants, I don't ask. I get to unbuckling."

"Fat Frank!" Melody chirped, and this time Frank had to look at her. "Please, everybody's just in boxers. And boxers are so *hip*." She stood and spun to show off her ensemble: a trim red blazer, and a white silk blouse tucked into oversize green-and-orange Miami Hurricanes boxers. She was a little less than half Frank's age, was a little more than a third of his weight, and had twice his hair, though hers was dyed. She had been at the station six months and had slept with as many men at the station during that time, if one believed the stories, which Frank did not. She was too lovely. Too—

Three minutes, said the voice in their ears.

Frank coughed. "Melody, my dear," he began—in a paternal voice. After all, she was half his age. That's why he carefully limited his fantasies of her to simplicities like a slow waltz across a darkened floor, the music swelling as the camera lingered. Father of the bride, perhaps? A favorite uncle? A beloved friend? He had not slept with anyone for four years, not since the "Amazing Alaska!" cruise he'd taken as a "Celebrity Guest!" And that woman was older—in bed, she proudly boasted of having the body of a sixty-year-old. Frank had previously taken her for fifty and, thinking on it now, realized she must have been at least seventy.

Melody looked at him, and he gripped the pen a little tighter, but who could see that?

"Don't you have to check your script?" he asked. "Read through it."

"They did it for me." Melody padded over to him, bare white feet slapping the slick black floor.

"*They* won't be going with you to your new job in Salt Lake." Frank listened to himself to make sure it sounded—what was it?—fatherly. He had no experience with situations like this—a bit of loveliness, live, beside him. His purest crushes—through his twenties, thirties, forties—had been with women on-screen, exclusively. No one in real life, on land or sea, ever looked so perfect, so irresistible—and he'd looked, some. But they had the wrong body, the wrong face, the wrong makeup. The lighting was always poor and the background noise just that, not music. And yet here, these last six months, had been someone more charming and sparkly than any star he'd seen in years. Right here, beside him, night after night, the cameras on. Here was a movie he'd finally been able to step into.

Melody moved closer, and now the distance between them could be measured in inches. Was Grace Kelly prettier? Maybe. But Grace had never whispered Frank's name, not while wearing boxers.

"Frank," Melody said quietly. She was one of the few who didn't insist on appending it with "Fat" *every* time, and Frank loved her for this alone. This, and the fact that she always smiled at him, always took pains to touch his forearm to make a point or say good-bye or hello or maybe just to make his heart seize up. Like now: she leaned over, bright eyes, bright teeth, soft lips, and whispered: "C'mon, drop 'em!" A shudder ran through Frank's chest and straight to the floor, and for a moment, he was unsure where his pants were—up, down, or back at home, in the closet, hanging neatly and patiently, awaiting his return.

Seats, please. Melody, we're starting with the fire, announced their IFBs.

"Did someone change the teleprompter?" she called, moving back behind the desk, her walk sure, her voice not. "Did you change it?"

You're going to go straight to Jeff for a live shot. Welcome, intro fire, intro Jeff. Ad-lib.

"Not in the 'prompter?" Melody called, studying her script.

Actually, the next line now was Frank's, and it wasn't for broadcast, but for Melody, a line of advice that had long ago been given to him: *remember, we had television before we had teleprompters.* Meaning, improvise. Meaning, make do.

Meaning, Frank realized yet again, that he was far, far older than Melody. So he said nothing and just looked at her. Though he promised himself he wouldn't, he looked at her legs, from where they emerged, smooth and pale from the boxer shorts, to where they turned at the knee, to where they ended, toes now tightly curled around the bottom rung of the swivel chair. She was chewing her pen.

"Grand slam, Joe," a crew member called out.

"Good golly," coughed Joe. The rule was no swearing on the set, even off-air; you never knew. It was regularly broken off-air, sometimes on-air, especially by Joe. He'd been warned, Frank knew. But Frank knew it was also partly why people watched: *what would Clean Joe Green do next?*

Right now, Joe was looking at Melody, who stared at a script, pen nervously in hand.

"You . . . want . . . me . . . to open?" Joe asked the ceiling, one eye still on Melody. "Big night for the Mariners. We get fires all the time."

No, Jeff's got a killer shot of a fireman rescuing this baby.

"Babies trump," said Joe, looking down.

"Tits, tots, pets, and vets!" shouted Melody. "The *T*'s of TV!"

And we're one minute out. Good show, everybody.

"Fluff!" swore Melody. Joe shook his head a bit and laughed, and Frank caught him leaning back, ever so slightly, for his own view of Melody's legs. Melody was still chewing her pen, still staring at her now outdated script. A crew woman in headphones pointed to the clock counting down on the wall behind the cameras.

"Melody," Frank whispered, low but forcefully. She looked at him and he touched his lips.

"No," she almost cried. Frank drew a finger along his own chin to show where her lipstick had smudged.

Thirty seconds.

Frank blinked awake, and quickly slid what he'd scribbled earlier over to Melody.

"WELCOME TO THE FIVE O'CLOCK NEWS. I'M MELODY ROGERS, HERE TONIGHT FOR ROGER WILKES. OUR TOP STORY, A HORRIFIC APARTMENT FIRE IN KINGSBURY'S HISTORIC DISTRICT. K-U-T-E REPORTER JEFF NELSON IS THERE. JEFF?"

Joe looked at Frank's note-passing and grinned; Melody just smiled wide, lifted her head, and spoke the lines just as Frank had written them, just as she was cued. Now Frank bit his lip, worried that "horrific" would throw her. When she delivered it, he could hear her not stumble over the word, but notice it, and he noticed her. No one else did.

Jeff was up on the monitor now, "reporting live," uncombed as usual, brow theatrically furrowed as usual. Frank looked for flames, but saw none. Finally, Jeff introed a tape from earlier, and they all sat back while it played.

"Death trap," said Joe.

"Cool shot, isn't it?" came Jeff's voice through their earpieces. Frank had never gotten used to the constant chatter in one ear, certainly not Jeff's chatter.

Where's the baby shot? someone asked.

"Coming up, coming up," Jeff said.

Have your outro?

"All set," Jeff said. "Melody, they drop trou for you?"

"Joe, yes; Frank, no." Melody shot Frank a pouty frown.

"Fire officials estimate the damage could run into the hundreds of thousands of dollars. But ask the families who lost their homes tonight, and they'll say what's gone . . . is priceless." Frank closed his eyes as a smoldering teddy bear came on-screen. "Reporting live, Jeff Nelson, KUTE News."

"Thanks, Jeff," Melody said. "We'll be back with weather, sports, news . . . and a movie review from KUTE's very own Fantastic Frank Douglas, right after this."

Clear. Back in ninety.

"That bear was so cute," Melody said. "So tragic." Frank shook his head. "Oh, c'mon Frank, you're just not being any fun at all tonight."

"Wait a second," said Joe. "Who the hell *is* doing weather? I didn't see Bernie in the newsroom."

"One rarely does," said Frank.

"Could be your big night, Fat Frank," Joe said. "'Cold front, over Topeka ...'"

"Please," said Frank.

"Oh my God!" Melody shouted. While the commercials rolled, the live-remote monitor showed Jeff Nelson, pantless but wearing a long fire coat, talking and laughing with some firemen.

"You *go*, Jeff," Joe said. "See that, Fat Frank? See that? Jeff, who ain't got *nothing* to show, he's dropped his pants for Melody." Jeff looked like he'd been rescued, his knobby knees and hairy calves peeking out from beneath the big reflective coat.

"You are so sweet, Jeff!" Melody shouted.

"I thought the inside joke was anchors *behind* the desk didn't wear pants," Frank said. "Which I actually *have* heard of happening, though usually in *smaller* markets."

No one was listening.

"Since we're off-air, can we get a close-up on those shorts?" Melody laughed, and Frank listened, carefully, hungrily, storing away every note in her voice, her laugh, its timbre, its sound. Too pretty.

Jeff did a little dance in front of the camera, which zoomed in on his rear. He, too, was wearing college underwear: Kentucky Wildcats. He turned around, and the camera focused on his crotch, where a catlike face appeared with the words, "Go big cats."

"Mee-ow," Melody purred.

Joe had been whispering with some of the crew; now, as one flashed him a thumbs-up, Joe deepened his voice a bit and imitated the producer: "Ahh, Jeff, hang on, we're going back to you live in five, four, three, two—"

"Fluff!" Jeff shouted. The camera shot opened wide, and Jeff dropped to a crouch, the coat gathered around him.

"Uh . . . snipers! Jeff Nelson, KUTE, here in Kingsbury's Historic

District, where unconfirmed reports of, um, sniper fire are, uh, affecting firemen's efforts to put out an earlier blaze."

Joe leaned back with a huge laugh and succeeded in crashing to the floor. A pair of techs ran up and righted him, checked his microphone and earpiece. Melody laughed through it all, but what Frank would remember, treasure, was the little sly look she gave him in the midst of the mess— Jeff ducking the "snipers" on the monitors in front of them, Joe helplessly giggling on the floor of the set. It was a look Frank had never seen before, and it meant everything. It was like an actor making an aside, but it wasn't just that. It was a shared bond, a connection, a common bemused disdain, and indulgent tolerance for all the foibles of this tiny station, this tiny town. It meant she really *knew* him, he thought. Like he knew her. One to one.

Two more news stories aired, and then a commercial break.

We're back in two minutes.

"Okay," Melody said, "who *is* doing the weather? Doesn't Bernie come on by now?"

We're looking for him. The voice sounded panicked, and shouting, with plenty of forbidden profanity, was ricocheting around the set's perimeter.

"Fall back plan is—?" Melody asked, getting nervous again. She and Frank looked at Joe.

"Oh, no," Joe said. "Only Fat Frank's got the pants for the weather walk, and besides, he's always tweaking me about pronouncing all those south county towns wrong."

"They notice," said Frank, soberly. It was no use fighting. Not Joe, nor the absent Bernie. He stood and walked toward the weather area; the job would fall to him.

"They should be glad they even get their assignations mentioned on my show," Joe said.

Quiet!

Frank now stood in front of the giant, blank light-green weather wall—which, to viewers at home, would soon appear to swirl with clouds and temperatures—while crew members fussed.

"Does this blazer button, Fat Frank?"

"You know how the clicker works?"

"You're just doing local and state. We'll keep it short and skip national, OK?"

Frank suffered it all with heavy sighs, eyes turned theatrically skyward. "Yes, yes."

"I would do it, Frank," Melody called over. "But I don't think it's right for the anchor, you know, to abandon his post."

"Her post," Frank offered gallantly.

"At least you wouldn't block out most of the western United States whenever you turned in profile," Joe said to Melody. "The southern parts, anyway." He leered. Melody smiled sweetly.

"We're certain Bernie's not coming?" Frank asked a final time.

Nice and short, Fat Frank. Sixty seconds. Just stick to your mark, keep it short, and toss it back to Melody for Joe's intro. OK, stand by.

"Last chance for the pants patrol," said Joe.

"Stuff it, you prattling monkey," said Frank. The lights were hotter in front of the weather wall.

"Oh, shut the fu—the fluff up," said Joe.

"Joe!" hissed Melody, before turning to the camera, just in time. "KUTE weatherman Bernie Dolan is, um, out sick tonight, so pinch-hitting is our very own Fantastic Frank Douglas. Frank, does this mean the weather's going to be, oh, fantastic as well?" As she spoke, she turned to face him full on, and Frank lost himself a moment in those bright eyes. She wore color-changing contacts, which also made her eyes water. On the set, she often looked as though she were ready to cry tears of joy over whatever she was about to say, or had just said. Frank wondered for a moment what his eyes looked like to her, or to Joe, or to the crew, or the guy at the dry cleaners, or the waitress at the twenty-four-hour diner he'd often frequent with a book, on sleepless nights. What did they see?

"Frank?" Melody asked.

"Well, sorry, *Melody*!" Frank roared to back to stage life. "I was just trying to think of another word for—FANTASTIC, but there it is, FANTASTIC. Here's hoping no one from out of state is watching tonight, because if word gets out how FANTASTIC it is around here, the place will be overrun! We're looking at seventy-five and sunny through the end of the week, overnight lows in the lower sixties. Up in the mountains, take it down about ten degrees, with midday highs around sixty, overnight lows in the upper forties. But still, beautiful early fall weather for northern Utah." Frank caught a glimpse of himself on the monitor and saw that he was pointing to Canada. "Not to mention for . . .

Sas-katchewan." He tried moving his hand down the blank wall, guiding himself with the monitor just off the set, but he kept caressing Canadian tundra; he couldn't figure out how to get his hand down to Kingsbury. So he put his hands in his pockets, and unconsciously began pointing out different spots with a jerk of his head, doing a quick weather recap for each. He smiled back at Melody. "And let's look at your Salt Lake City weather, since that's where KUTE's own Melody Rogers will be heading later this week." Melody gave Frank a sad smile, which shook Frank to such a degree that he simply said, "Warm and pleasant, and I hear the people are, too."

"Thanks, Fantastic Frank, that's sweet," Melody said.

Frank ached from head to toe—standing there, under the lights, doing weather, losing Melody—it made him generally ill.

"How about Bernie, F-F-Frank?" Joe put on a manic smile. "What do you think the weather's like where he is?"

"He's at home sick," Melody interrupted.

"Oh, if he's where I think he is," Frank said, "he's roasting."

"We'll be right back with Clean Joe Green's Sports Scene in just a moment," Melody said.

Clear. Back in sixty. Soft intro, sports, dog show, Fat Frank, and out.

"Frank, you were awesome," Melody said. Frank gave a courtly nod, and limped regally back to his seat. "You should do weather all the time," she added. "But I guess it's no fun standing." Frank offered a tight smile. "What's the limp from, anyway?" she asked.

"Honey," Joe answered, "you can't carry 400 pounds on two knees and not wobble a little." Frank opened his mouth to correct Joe, but 280 didn't sound much better than 400, so he gestured weakly and sat back.

"Hey guys," Melody shouted skyward, "I've got to take a potty break."

No time, the answer came, but Melody was already moving. Crew chased after to make sure she was unhooked. Joe darted over to Frank.

"Sign this, Fat Frank," Joe whispered, looking after Melody. A fuzzy, sad-looking dog cartoon appeared on the front of the card: "Dog-gone," it read. Frank opened it. "We're sorry to see a good dog go."

"Good dog?" Frank asked.

"Just sign it. And we're having a little surprise party for the kid right after, over on the cooking-show set." Frank read the different inscriptions—"You go, girl," "Don't forget us!" *"Vaya con Dios, senorita!"*—the last of which seemed to be Joe's addition. Frank uncapped his pen, and to annoy Joe, took a leisurely moment to begin writing, though he knew what he would say.

"Just write something," Joe said. Frank looked at him blankly, and lowered his gaze to Joe's polka dot boxers. Joe involuntarily crossed his legs. "They glow," Joe said. "The dots."

"Handy," Frank said. He looked at the card again. *"Have a Fantastic Future!"* he signed quickly, adding the same signature he put on publicity photos: "FF." Melody ran back in, and Joe snatched the card away. As Frank watched him go, he slipped a hand into his breast pocket to make sure *his* card was still there. He surreptitiously slid out the buff-colored envelope, and rubbed it gently between thumb and forefinger. It was beautiful stationery, specially ordered. Reading what was written on the front—"Melody"—reminded him of his hour-long debate: blue ink or black, blue or black, the two smudged attempts with blue, and this final, clean version in black. He'd drawn a little line under her name, as though it were a careless afterthought, and now he wondered if it was.

"Give me something on those Mariners," shouted Joe.

"I'm ready," said Melody, shooting a bright smile at Frank, and then turning to Joe. "What do you want me to say?"

"Ask me about the Dodgers," Joe said, not looking up.

Thirty seconds.

"The Dodgers?" Melody asked. She looked at Frank, who shook his head and mouthed, "No." Melody's face contorted in some alarm. "Mariners," Frank mouthed, but Melody shook her head frantically: *Yes, Mariners, but what about them?*

"Good evening, I'm Melody Rogers, in the anchor chair tonight for Roger Wilkes. Well, Joe, how about those—" She cocked her head a moment, and Joe looked at her smiling, giving away nothing. Frank was willing the words, transmitting them telepathically, staring them into the back of her head. "How did the Mariners get their name?" Melody asked weakly.

"How did who?" Joe asked, laughing.

"The Mariners," Melody repeated, substituting a goofy smile for poise.

"Who knows, Melody, but they're getting a better name tonight after their performance at home in Seattle. Let's take a look, here in the first inning . . ."

Melody stood up and wandered over to Frank while the game highlights played.

"He can be so mean," Melody said.

"He's harmless," Frank said. "How are you feeling?" He lost his voice, found it. "Sad? Nostalgic? Excited?"

"Nervous, I guess. This is my big chance, you know. The woman I'm replacing went to *Los Angeles*. But I can't think about that, not yet."

"Well," Frank said and paused. He got ready to say it: *We'll miss you*. But Melody spoke first.

"So what about the pants, Frank?" Melody asked.

"Melody, dear, I can't. Some of us look attractive in shorts"—he gestured vaguely at her, refusing to look down—"some of us look better in pants. I am among the panted."

"Oh Frank, everybody looks foolish. It's just a joke. You know, so you can say one day, 'Oh yes, I once did the news bottomless.'"

"Say that to whom?"

"You big sourpuss," Melody said, smiling, and tugged at one

of his pant legs, just below the knee. Frank held his breath, and kept holding it, until she'd straightened up and walked back to her chair.

"That's not all the sports news for today," Melody was saying. "Today was the fifth annual Flying Dog Open out at Title Creek Park." On the screen, dogs leapt into the air and caught Frisbees under Kodachrome skies. "Dozens of canines competed for the Top Dog award, and in this competition, being at the top means being very high indeed." She'd mistimed it, and the shot of a dog soaring over a man's outstretched arm ran by before she finished. "We'll be right back with Fantastic Frank's movie roundup, right after this."

We're clear.

"Sorry about the dogs," Melody called out. "Did you catch that?" she asked no one in particular.

"Those animals are incredible," Joe said. "And did you see, Frank? Not a one of them wearing pants."

Frank was toiling over his script, doing math in the margins. How far was it to Salt Lake? Four hours? Three? He remembered jumping station to station in his youth, like Melody, up the ladder one rung at a time, until he'd gotten to Kingsbury—and then what? Just stopped climbing? Why? Why didn't he go to Salt Lake City? Or Phoenix, or Chicago, for that matter? Or gone all the way—Los Angeles, New York? He'd gotten too heavy to climb, Joe would say. And maybe that was part of it. But Kingsbury was friendly, easy. It had its quiet pleasures. It didn't have much in the way of culture, but that could be had via catalogs, press junkets, vacations, movies. If you had to live somewhere alone, this was a good place. Good enough.

All of a sudden, Melody was saying, "To finish up tonight, we go to our very own Fantastic Frank Douglas for a quick look at the week at the movies. Frank?"

Startled, Frank thanked her, but moved smoothly through his script. Current releases, new releases, videos. Everything got a good review; even his warnings to parents about non-kid-friendly movies were apologetic. After his final "fantastic," it was good-bye, good-night, and someone popped a cork in the cooking-show kitchen just seconds before they went off the air. The final wide shot caught all of them looking surprised and laughing, even Frank.

"Good show!" shouted Melody once they were off-air.

"Good enough!" shouted Joe. "Fiesta!"

Frank slipped away to take off his makeup, and the party began.

When Frank returned, he surveyed what Joe had laid in for the festivities: two bags of chips, three cases of beer, a fifth of vodka, another of tequila, and a bottle of Cook's California champagne. Still, Melody seemed very pleased, very flattered, and was on her way to becoming very drunk.

"We still have an eleven o'clock wrap-up to do," shouted Joe with a laugh and a beer raised high. Melody clinked bottles with him.

"Fat Frank!" Melody all but screamed. "C'mon, join my *party*." Frank held up a single finger, and lumbered stiffly off. He returned a few minutes later with a couple of bottles of pinot noir he'd spotted in *Wine Spectator* a few months back. He did not know if Melody knew wine, but he liked the idea of introducing her to it if she didn't.

"*Laissez les bon temps rouler,*" he announced and held the bottles aloft in what he felt was a jaunty, open manner. Joe rolled his eyes; Melody didn't see him. She was sitting on the kitchen island, a beer in her hand, her legs swinging back and forth. Frank opened one of the bottles and dribbled some out into a plastic tumbler.

Additional chips arrived, then pizza, and then additional alcohol. By nine, most of the crowd was drunk and pantless. Frank had long since stopped worrying about whether they'd be ready for the eleven o'clock; unable to find takers for his wine, he'd finished one bottle himself and had made a good start on the second. He was feeling fine and, for a change, *light*, buoyed not so much by the wine—or so he convinced himself—but the thought that something good was happening. A young woman with a good future was getting a start on that future. Fine. Frank forced a flush of professional pride and, with the help of the wine, almost succeeded. He'd carried on conversations with a number of people at the party he'd never spoken to before, and it seemed as though they'd talked of great, grand things. At the start of the party, he'd longed to sweep Melody off her feet, and twirl her about the floor between the cameras and the anchor desk while the cameras looked on admiringly. But his desires mellowed with the wine, the conversation, and conviviality. Now it was enough to stand and talk and smile nearby; every so often he'd touch his chest with what he hoped looked like an absent air, and feel the envelope, the note, still resting there, and take a deep breath.

And now people *were* dancing, Frank realized. Music was coming from somewhere, some pulsing, electronic hoo-ha. Before,

Joe had eagerly whispered that he'd remembered to bring his Sinatra CD, so Frank had better get ready for the final "New York, New York" kick line. But this was not Sinatra playing, not yet. Frank searched the dance floor for Melody, but she was arm-wrestling some guy on the kitchen's cutting board. Joe, however, was leaping about to the music with the older woman from the tape library; two men from the crew were slamming into each other, falling down, and then getting up to go again. Frank took it all in, sipping and nodding, always keeping an eye on the dancers.

Legs were fascinating: they came in all shapes, muscular and thin, thick and veined, hairy, smooth, scarred, clear. Someone had broken into the promotions closet, it seemed, because almost everyone was wearing leftover KUTE gym shorts from last year's celebrity hoops challenge. Frank was certain there were none in his size, but stopped short when he realized he was even entertaining the thought. He set his mouth into a grim line and swallowed the last of the wine.

Then he saw her. Fluttering across the floor like clothes on a line, Melody, untucked, bounced from dancer to dancer as the music throbbed. Frank watched her carefully, crossly, until Joe appeared at his side.

"OK, fat guy. You got pants on, but that doesn't mean you can't dance."

"I can't dance, Joseph," Frank said, bending down to tell Joe this, surprised to feel dizzy as he did so.

"Please, Fat Frank, I see three-hundred-pound linemen dance on the football field all the time. Bum leg or no, just get out there and swing. Show the kid a good time," Joe said and slammed his hand down on the counter. One of the wine bottles rolled off and clattered on the floor, unbroken. "Shhhhoofly," slurred Joe.

Frank threaded his way to the center, feeding off the shouts of "Fat Frank! Fat Frank!" that sprang up all around him. Melody spun over to him, smiling crazily. Frank looked away for a moment; she was too lovely. When he looked back, she was sashaying up against him, and Frank began to rock his shoulders in what felt like hepcat fashion, keeping his feet rooted to the floor. Melody reached up and clumsily loosened his tie; his instinct was to interfere, but the wine conspired with her charm to render him powerless. So, too, was he unable to stop his belt from being unbuckled, and from sliding out from around his waist. Melody caught her tongue between her teeth, and looked up, a wild look. The crowd hooted and cheered. Terror swelled up from somewhere within Frank, but he was too happy; Melody was having too much fun. It was like a lurid moment in a movie that he'd intended to fast-forward past but instead found himself watching, remote in hand, waiting.

And besides, it was just his belt.

He heard Joe behind him: "Fat Frank, your moment is here!" Frank felt Joe's fingers dig into his pockets, and suddenly yank down. Frank finally panicked as he remembered that these were his new pants, specially tailored for a loose fit, the first pair that had fit him comfortably in two years. They came straight down.

Melody screamed.

Joe swore.

Frank bent over to snatch up his pants, but they snagged on the knee joint of his prosthetic left leg. The leg was new; the old one had gotten heavier and heavier, it seemed. He was still going back and forth with the doctors on adjustments for this one, so they hadn't fleshed it yet. The reflected glare of the studio lights was almost blinding to anyone who looked at the leg's titanium gleam, as most everyone did, except for

Melody. Frank thought he heard one of the crew say, "Fan-*tas*-tic!"

Joe fumbled down, and gently helped Frank pull his pants back up. But they kept snagging, and eventually, Frank leaned on Joe—to such a degree that Joe couldn't move—and kicked off one pant leg, then the other. At least he'd worn the dark-blue plaid boxers from Brooks Brothers. Melody stood with her back against the anchor desk.

Frank walked over to Melody, staring into her face, waiting to catch her gaze. "Melody," he said boozily when he'd reached her.

"I'm—I'm, oh Frank." She was crying a bit now, desperately not looking.

The music was softer now, everything was.

"Care—to—trip—the light fantastic?" He was shocked to hear the words sound as sulky and awkward as he felt, because he'd rehearsed them in daydreams a dozen times before, before he ever knew there would be an opportunity to ask. But in rehearsal, the words were delivered with a smile and answered with one; he was wearing pants but no prosthesis. In rehearsal, he had two fine legs and danced like a star.

"Hey, Frank." Joe came around between Frank and Melody, weaving a bit, and punched Frank lightly on the shoulder. "You old dog, keeping this a secret." Frank imagined Joe dropping to the floor, unconscious. Instead, Joe looked at Melody: "Go ahead, kid, a dance with Mr. Fantastic." Melody wouldn't look at either of them, and ran from the room. Frank felt his breathing quicken and quicken until he realized he was crying.

"Put on my goddamned CD!" Joe shouted. "Frank," he said softly. "She's a silly little girl. They're going to eat her alive down in Vegas." *Salt Lake City,* Frank thought, and just stood there. In the movie, he would sob, but this wasn't a movie, he wasn't a star, and Melody wasn't an object. She was a person and he was a person and this was a dance. Which must have been why, as "The Way You Look Tonight" began ringing through the room, Joe moved close and gathered as much of Frank up as he could into an embrace.

They began to sway with the music. Frank kept his eyes shut tight, no longer able to watch whatever happened. All those faces. All those legs. Sinatra sang song after song, and Frank tried to rearrange the night, the months that Melody had been in Kingsbury, the years that he had been here. He imagined different openings, different endings, and sifted through different soundtracks. Sinatra would do fine, he thought.

This song—now it was "Fly Me to the Moon"—would do fine. Let the camera drift back and away, he thought, and saw the shot: circling up to the ceiling, holding at center just the two of them standing there, he and Joe, swaying, until a scent, a touch, a voice, a whisper—"Mind if I cut in?"—and two thin arms reaching around him, a head falling to his chest. And who could say? Eyes closed against the crowd, Frank couldn't see Joe, his own leg, their legs, or Melody standing there, leaning against him, moving with him, his note to her pressed between them, all of it possible, invisible, fantastic.

Flush

SOMEONE WOULD BE ALONG TO UNLOCK THE MAUSOLEUM SHORTLY. Surely. Julia knew this. Matthias had said this and Julia had believed him, because what was the other option? That she'd spend the rest of her time in Berlin—the rest of her life?—underground in Treptower Park with five thousand dead Soviet soldiers? Not likely.

She watched Matthias, the tour guide, recheck the door that had closed on them and locked. Like a bad movie, this, or a good one, actually, because other than the self-locking door, there were plenty of unique elements.

There was the location itself, the Sowjetisches Ehrenmal, an immense memorial-mausoleum in southeastern Berlin where the Russians had buried their dead after the liberation of the city in World War II.

There was Matthias, their tour guide, who had confessed to Julia early on that he was a cellist, that he'd taken this job because a promised gig with a new opera company hadn't panned out. Then the other member of the tour—a dad—had called over with a question about the Brandenburg Gate, and Julia had gotten a good look at the back of Matthias's neck and the starting-to-be-long brown hair that was attempting to obscure it. Matthias was handsome.

And there was Arthur, her boyfriend, who'd parked her on this tour while he spent the day in Potsdam researching German hyperinflation of the 1930s. If the door to the mausoleum had clicked shut, she was locked in, but it was equally true that Arthur was locked out. She'd asked Arthur about his research and he shook his head: she couldn't understand, her German wasn't good enough. But she did understand. She'd seen the photographs of 1930s Germans pushing around wheelbarrows full of almost-worthless deutschmarks. Hyperinflation.

It's not that simple, Arthur had said and tried to run his tongue between her breasts one last time. Maybe she shouldn't have asked when they were naked. Maybe she shouldn't have been thinking about hyperinflation during lovemaking. But what else was there? There was Arthur, licking away, leaving her feeling like a giant glazed doughnut, or *Berliner*—or maybe a pancake, *Pfannkuchen* since that's what Arthur said Berliners called themselves. Either way: sticky.

"I have a cell phone," the father said, going into his fanny pack—which, though this was the tenth time she'd seen him rustle through the thing, still made her think, for a split second, that he was undoing his fly. She looked away. He'd find the phone soon enough; everything was in there. They'd be rescued shortly.

It was just the three of them on the tour, she, Matthias, and the dad. The dad said he had wanted to have his family along, but his wife and daughters had rebelled. Julia figured they didn't share the dad's delight in all things technological—this was a Segway Urban Adventure, and so each of them got to use a Segway for the duration of the tour. "Cover twice the Berlin in half the time!" promised the flyer Arthur had shoved at her.

Julia had a cell phone, too, but Arthur had told her not to use it, since international roaming was expensive.

Matthias shook his head.

"Just tell me who to call," the father said. It was odd not to know his name, but of course Julia hadn't told him hers. Now that they were trapped underground, it would be inevitable, she thought, that they'd exchange names. But how?

"It is not easy," said Matthias.

The father held out the phone. "Okay, you do it." Julia half liked the dad, even his stub of a ponytail. He was amenable to anything, not your usual American in Europe. Maybe he was Canadian.

"No," said Matthias. "The problem is—the problem is, we are not supposed to be here."

"Ah." The father looked at Julia. "What do you make of this?"

Julia looked around. They were just inside the locked doorway in a small vestibule. The tour's theme had been "hidden Berlin." They had seen a lot of blank-front apartment blocks that Matthias claimed contained former safe houses or secret prisons.

"We must wait," said Matthias.

That made no sense; Julia assumed he was just trying to get back at her. She'd been the one who'd tried the door, peeked inside. It had been hot and oppressive in the middle of the vast, sunken memorial court the Soviets had built, marbled quotes from Stalin (in Russian and

German) pressing in from all sides. But at one end there had been a door, and it had opened for her, and they had followed her, and the door had closed behind them. She'd only wanted to escape for a moment.

The father reached again into his fanny pack and brought out a tiny deck of cards: "Just the thing."

Julia looked at Matthias, but Matthias merely closed his eyes and nodded, as though the father had produced a gun, that it had come to this, that they would die, one by one.

Matthias looked so woebegone, in fact, that Julia looked again at the father's hands: nope, just a deck of cards.

"I think we should keep going," Julia said quickly. The cards were creepy. "What's in there?" She pointed to a door farther on, opposite the one that had shut on them.

"Dead soldiers," the father said and turned back to Matthias.

"I will call my girlfriend," Matthias said, giving Julia and the dad separate reasons to dislike him.

"Not the police?" said the dad, smiling.

"As I say," began Matthias.

"Your girlfriend has a key?" asked the dad.

"She is very smart, and—" Matthias looked at Julia.

Do I remind him of her? Julia thought. No, I'm an improvement on her. And no matter. The girlfriend: she is outside, with Arthur, roaming Germany. Maybe the two of them would meet up, fall in love, get married.

"And what?" the father asked.

"She will come and get us out?" Matthias seemed unsure of the plan or the vocabulary.

"She has a key?" repeated the father.

"Maybe she does not need the key," said Matthias, still uncertain. "And if get us out she cannot, she can call the boss."

"Let's start with your boss," the dad said, only now putting the cards away.

Arthur had been her RA in school. He was on their floor all the time; her neighbors included several members of the football team who were always getting drunk, getting in trouble. At their school, football was only a club sport. Arthur thought that was why they *acted out*. Julia had liked that, the explanation and the childcare terminology. And she'd liked Arthur, too. It hadn't been head over heels or anything, but she'd actually thought that a good sign. Here was a boy she could be rational about, who was responsible and tended to her, who was attractive, in his way. He was tall and thin and—they'd never talked about it, but she could tell—bad at sports. The football guys would have flattened him on the field.

He wasn't like the other RAs. He was a grad student, in history, and that had appealed to her, too. A grown-up, for a change. She'd actually dated one of the football guys for a while. Dated: like they'd ever gone on a date. Still, "fooled around with" seemed too temporary a term for something that had lasted an entire semester. He got drunk every Thursday and Saturday—he actually had a schedule—and Julia had liked that Arthur almost never got drunk, and if he did, it was completely unplanned.

She didn't think he'd planned, for example, to get drunk that last night in the dorm—everyone gone, just Julia and Arthur and three of the football players all set to leave for summer. Everyone had to be out by seven the next morning.

The label said they were drinking bourbon; it was a bottle someone had found in an empty room. No one had money left to go buy anything else. Julia took little sips or passed on the bottle altogether, but Arthur drank deeply, and eventually suggested the game switch from penny stakes to clothing. *Strip poker,* which made Julia smile, a smile the boys all misinterpreted. Because it was just a private joke with her; in high school, she'd thought—she'd feared—that college would be one long, nonstop session of strip poker. She'd gleaned this from books and movies. Comic exaggerations, she knew, but they'd had to start from a grain of truth, right? Or so she'd thought. Still, she'd taught herself to play poker, online. She'd gotten good. She'd never played with people, not since.

Now, in the dorm, she was starting the game at a deficit; unlike the boys, she wasn't wearing socks and shoes, or, she realized, discreetly fingering an earlobe, earrings. She hoped they wouldn't notice that she'd checked.

It hardly took half an hour for her to have all the boys in their underwear. The football guys, who weren't nearly as fit as they apparently thought, all pressed to go on. Julia would have. It wasn't about the sex—*sorry, guys*—it was so very much about the beautiful cards, about making them do just what she wanted them to, about knowing what was going to appear before someone displayed a hand. It was about winning.

But she'd called it quits for Arthur. The loss of his clothes had laid bare a pale stripling of a man. He'd run out of clean laundry—he didn't normally wear briefs, honest, he usually wore boxers. It didn't matter; he'd looked like an infant and they had laughed, all of them. He had both too little hair and too much, so black against his skin. Two a.m., he'd knocked on her door—*to apologize*—and she'd kissed him and they'd been going out ever since.

Julia watched now as Matthias called his girlfriend, not his boss. The girlfriend wasn't there. He left a voice mail. The father looked at his watch. The room was cool, but strangely not damp.

Matthias called again five minutes later: another voice mail.

"She is in class," he told Julia.

He wasn't that handsome, Julia decided.

"I'm going to call my boyfriend," Julia said, but Matthias only shrugged. Julia had asked Arthur if there were a better word in German for *boyfriend*; she didn't like the English word at all. Both halves—*boy, friend*—smacked of playground, elementary school.

He'd said he'd ask.

Julia dialed. After a series of rapid rings, intelligible as a sign of trouble even to someone who had never heard them before, a recorded voice, female, German, came on. Julia hung up and wondered how much it had cost.

The dad did his fanny pack thing again and fished out his phone, checked it. "I'm not getting a signal." Julia got ready to tell him that he couldn't use hers.

But he didn't ask. He redeposited his phone and glanced around. "Let's look around. What the hell."

The door that led deeper within was secured with a rusty padlock, but when the dad went to check it, the entire latch came away in his hand. Something gently blew the door open, and the dad looked back at them, leaving it ajar.

"Sure," Julia said and looked at Matthias. He shook his head, and then shrugged.

"What's in there?" the dad said.

"I don't know," Matthias said. "Maybe there was another door we were supposed to go in, somewhere in the park. I don't think we're supposed to be here. There's supposed to be an exhibit. A small exhibit."

"This does not look small," said the dad. He opened the door farther, and a deep cold came around all of them. The vestibule where they'd been standing had been lit, dimly, by sunlight that leaked around the door to the outside. This new space beyond, though, was perfectly dark.

"Do you have a flashlight?" the dad asked.

Matthias shook his head, no, in relief.

The dad reached into the pack. "I do, but it's a small one."

It was about the size of his pinky, and when he shone it inside, it did nothing to disperse the dark. But after a moment, he said, "Aha" and, with a grinding crunch, apparently turned a switch.

A series of lights bloomed on, illuminating a vast underground cavern. After a second or two, several of the lights started popping—one, two, three, four—each turning a brief, bright blue before zapping into darkness.

It made for a spectacular display; it was as if the room shook with light, and when the explosions stopped, it took their eyes some time to adjust to the yellowy twilight that remained, along with a loud, electric humming.

"Wow," Julia said, or tried to say, but her mind didn't seem set on the word, and so she simply mouthed it.

"I think we're in bigger trouble now," the dad said.

"Or Matthias is." Julia picked her way past him, through the door.

She stood at the top of a metal spiral staircase and looked out over the room. It was hard to say for sure, but the space appeared as long and as broad as a football field. The ceiling was supported by a series of cement arches, leaving the center free of pillars.

Matthias had said the Soviets had lost twenty thousand troops in the battle for Berlin. Five thousand were buried at the memorial. But where? This looked like a—

"You're going to tell us not to go in," the dad said. The dad was speaking to Matthias but looking at Julia, then at the cavern. (The tomb?) Then Julia.

There was no reply, but Julia could almost hear Matthias give another of his wordless shrugs.

The three stood at the top of the metal staircase for a long moment until Julia spoke: "What's with the desks, Matthias?"

Matthias came forward.

"Where?" said the dad, unnecessarily—there were desks everywhere. One set ran along the outside walls of the room, and another set, grouped in pairs of two, formed an interior circle.

Julia started down the stairs.

"Rats," Matthias said.

She stopped.

"I don't see any rats," the dad said, though he didn't move, either.

"Rats," Matthias said. "Is this the word?"

Julia kept going down.

"And guns?" the dad said. "Those are rifles? Machine guns?"

They had to adjust how they walked—the dust, or dirt, lay almost an inch thick on the floor, and kicking through it created clouds that hung solidly in place, in no hurry to dissipate. Julia was the one who came up with the best method, a kind of slow, balletic step, each foot carefully raised and placed.

The dad's theory was that the tomb, the memorial above, was a grand con; this was actually an underground bunker—the word soon became his favorite, *bunker,* and he worked it into almost everything he ever said after—a place where the East Germans could wait out nuclear annihilation above and subsequently reemerge to take over the world.

Julia's theory, unvoiced, was that this was a tomb of the ancient-civilization variety, the Soviets taking a page from Tutankhamen and burying themselves with all that they might need for the next world: soldiers, guns. Desks.

"We should stop here," Matthias said. He put a hand out toward Julia. She watched it, and then watched it fall.

"What if there's another way out of the bunker?" the dad said.

"Does your phone work down here?" Julia asked.

"Mine didn't work up there," the dad said. "I'm sure it wouldn't work down here in *das Bunker,* either."

"*Der Bunker,*" Matthias said and checked his phone. Julia could tell by his face that it worked.

"No signal," he said, snapping it shut.

"And you," the dad asked. "What about yours?"

She looked at it, stared at it, in fact, because it was showing she had an incoming call. Somehow, the phone had toggled itself to silent ring—the screen flashed, once, twice. She answered it: her dad.

Carefully stepping away, Julia explained to her dad, yet again, that Arthur had asked that the phone be used only for emergencies. International roaming, after all, was expensive and—and her dad cut her off, yet again, and asked her to tell Arthur to fuck off. Her father also promised to cover the cost of the call.

"When are you coming home?" he asked.

"Arthur's getting good work done." She looked at the dad, who was drawing a finger along the surface of a desk. Not as dirty as she'd thought. She wanted to sit on it and did. This desk had a phone. It was lettuce green, and had nothing on its face, no dial, no buttons. She wanted to pick it up.

"But you're not. It's September 30, Jules," he said. "School started four weeks ago."

"I—"

"I know, because they sent a bill. And I paid it."

"This isn't a good time to talk, Dad," Julia said, looking around at Matthias. It was going to be just as awkward, she realized, telling her Dad that she was breaking things off with Arthur, even worse than the conversation she'd previously been practicing, that they'd eloped.

"It's a great time," her dad said.

"My battery is dying."

"Come home. Now."

"Dad," Julia said.

"You're not unreachable. Arthur—Arthur has a family, too, right? I'll call them."

"Tomorrow, Dad."

"Tomorrow. We'll talk, same time, and I'll give you the address of the American Express office. I talked to them today. They'll have money and a ticket for you. Thank God."

"Dad."

"Arthur can figure out his own goddamned way home."

"Okay."

"Or he can stay."

She stayed silent.

"Julia?"

"Okay," she said and hung up.

Matthias looked away.

The dad stared straight at her.

"It's only because he loves you." He smiled. "Even with you buried in a bunker, he loves you."

"Thanks," she said.

"Here's the plan," the dad said, as though he and Matthias had been plotting while she was on the phone. He undid his fanny pack and set it on a desk. "We're going to go back up to the door, the locked door, and give it a shove. A good hard one. If it's cheaply made as everything else, it'll pop open."

Julia waited. This wasn't a plan. After it had shut on them, they'd all thrown themselves against the door, first the boys, then her, then together. It hadn't budged. It had seemed rather well made.

Matthias nodded.

"I'll wait here," Julia said.

"Why?" the dad said.

"I'll wait with her," Matthias suddenly said.

The dad looked at them, frowned, and picked his way back to the stairs. Naïve, determined, the little cloud at his feet: he looked very much like the Charlie Brown character. Which character, though? She wanted to ask Matthias. But he wouldn't know. Idiot. Still, he'd opted to stay with her.

Once she thought of the name, she wanted to brush away a bit of Matthias's hair, whisper it in his ear.

It was very straightforward to get an abortion in Germany, Arthur had explained. And the health care was *top notch*. Julia wondered if that was a term Matthias knew, *top notch*. She also wondered if Matthias would, at some point, kiss her, or she him, or she the dad, or maybe even the dad and Matthias would kiss. It would be nice for someone to kiss someone here in the tomb. The abortion had been scheduled for last Friday, then Monday, then today, until Arthur finally said, *I think you need time to think.*

"Where is he?" Matthias asked and nodded to the top of the stairs.

For a moment, Julia didn't say anything. She tried to figure out how Arthur had found her, what she would say to him.

But there was no one at the top of the stairs, and Matthias was talking about the dad. She felt like she'd been sleeping for days and, looking at Matthias, realized that was what had drawn her to him, that he looked the way she felt, exhausted, excited.

"I don't know." Julia looked back up to the top of the stairs. "I haven't heard anything. Maybe he got out?"

She thought of the dad speeding away on one of Segways. They were very lifelike, the scooters. If you stepped off them, they quivered for a bit, as if wondering where the weight had gone. They were probably frantic by now, come to think of it.

"I'm so sorry," Matthias said, looking suddenly miserable.

"It's okay." She put out a hand to his forearm, lightly, not so much to be tender, but out of habit, as if afraid that he, like everything else in the cavern, was liable to kick up a cloud of dust if disturbed too much.

"No one will know?" he asked, and Julia shook her head, and then nodded, not sure which was the best way to agree: *No, no one will find out what a lousy tour guide you are. You'll keep your job until your next cellist gig comes through.*

He kissed her. Very lightly, on her hand, as lightly as she'd touched him. She watched quietly and did not pull her hand away.

He kissed her forearm next, and that was too much. She pulled her arm away, and he looked up, less stricken than resigned.

"You're not a musician," she said. "The cello?"

He looked at her blankly. Then he leaned in to kiss her again.

"This is your real job," she said, working it out. "Tour guide."

"No," he said and tried kissing her hand again. She let him. His lips were very soft. He might be much younger than she'd thought: not her age, maybe a mere teenager.

She adjusted herself on the desk and Matthias leaned closer. But something fell as she moved and they broke off. It was the fanny pack, left behind. Matthias picked it up off the floor and handed it to Julia. She smiled and unzipped it. Cigarettes, the phone, the cards, no wallet, gum, a prescription. A condom. A laminated photo of a woman, dark haired, not smiling, in a blue bikini against a sunny cinder block wall. No pictures of kids.

Matthias wasn't a tour guide, the dad wasn't a dad, Arthur wasn't her boyfriend, and someone had turned a memorial to the dead into Cold War office space. She was pregnant and would remain so, she would kiss Matthias and never see him again, they would be rescued soon. She would go to the American Express office, take the money, cash in the ticket, and retreat, with the Soviets, farther east. Tomorrow.

Now? The dad was returning, looking at her unevenly as she held his fanny pack in her hands. Matthias looked at him as though he were Julia's dad and blushed. Julia smiled and took out the cards.

"I can't get the door open," the father said in a very unfatherly voice.

"That's okay," Julia said.

She swept a hand across the desktop where she'd kissed Matthias. She undid the zipper, emptied the pack's contents across the desk, found the cards, looked up, and, finally, smiled.

"I'll deal."

Exhibit A

By day thirty-seven, he'd broken dozens of rules, so what was one more? He went up and introduced himself to the woman in front of the Soyuz space capsule.

"My name's Phil," he said. It wasn't. He extended a hand.

It took a moment, but she extended hers, and gave her name, which he immediately replaced with "Amber," because he wasn't about to break *that* rule: *Never use visitors' real names.*

His was Elliot, and he wrote the museum's *Above and Beyond* blog from a twelve-foot-diameter glass sphere suspended near the Tesla coil. He'd lived there for weeks now, having won a fifty-word essay contest. Every day at eleven and three, he opened a hatch and descended a ladder to answer questions and use the bathroom.

At night, he was to stay put.

As were special nighttime event attendees—and they usually did, sticking to the Hall of Flight downstairs, a room that had become increasingly attractive to caterers: additional floor space kept opening as the struggling museum sold off historic aircraft. Although guests sometimes wandered beyond the ropes, no night visitor had ever wandered before this far into his wing, the Hall of Wonders, which Elliot had overheard a curator describe as the museum's junk drawer. There was a deep-sea diver's bathysphere (with the otherwise misplaced Soyuz nearby for comparison), a fist-sized green space rock, an ant farm, a timeline of adhesives and another of artificial fabrics, a Plexiglas beehive connected to the roof by a clear pipe that was cloudy with wax and pollen, and, of course, Elliot's "blogosphere," which perched next to—

"Wow," Amber said, staring not at the blogosphere, but the neighboring exhibit, the Tesla coil, Elliot's rival. The coil sparked purple spasms inside its own glass sphere all day long, drawing visitors away from him; at night, when it was supposed to be off, it continued to crack and buzz and affect his laptop, whose display had compressed itself into a two-inch column of cowering pixels.

Maybe his brain had been fritzed, too. Because Elliot now heard himself do something else he shouldn't have, which was invite the woman on a "behind-the-scenes tour." He told her he'd found a hidden door, a hidden catwalk, a hidden exhibit in the rafters high above the Hall of Flight.

(And Elliot had. It was dizzying to tell the truth, however briefly.)

"I should get back to the party," Amber said. It was a summer gathering for high schoolers interested in attending private, college-level military academies. She was close to graduating from one out west, she explained. She looked down the hall. She was as tall as he was. Taller. Definitely smarter. She turned back to him.

Elliot could tell she was up to something, but he couldn't quite say what. That wasn't Tesla's fault, or maybe it was. After hours, Elliot had a lot of free time to roam and read. So he'd learned that in 1934, at age seventy-eight, Nikola Tesla had announced the invention of an electronic apparatus so strong it could "bring down a fleet of 10,000 enemy airplanes at a distance of 250 miles," or so the *New York Times* reported. (Tesla called it a "death-beam." The *New York Sun*, a "peace ray.") An editorial in the British *Electrical Review*, meanwhile, mused that "Mr. Tesla may be quite invulnerable to Cupid's shafts" but that "science in general, and Mr. Tesla in particular, will be all the richer when he gets married." Did studies bear this out? Did British journal editors often cite Cupid? Unclear. Two things were certain, though: Tesla never did marry. And the man loved pigeons. So much so that he fed "thousands of them for years," Tesla later told the science writer for the *Times,* adding, "There was one, a beautiful bird, pure white with light grey tips on its wings; that one was different. It was a female. I had only to wish and call her and she would come flying to me. I loved that pigeon as a man loves a woman, and she loved me. . . . As long as I had her, there was a purpose to my life."

Elliot thought that Tesla, and his coil, were crazy and that pigeons were dirty. But like Tesla, he was suspicious of marriage. Unlike Tesla, he had once proposed.

"You—your—it's a very cool uniform," Elliot said. A floor-length dress paired with a tiny, unbuttonable tunic, it reminded him of both Ulysses S. Grant and Mary Todd Lincoln, as though each had been caught halfway through trying on the other's outfit.

But Amber's V-shaped tie reminded him of neither Grant nor Lincoln. Upside-down and thus pointing to her face, the V worked like any other of the hundreds of directional arrows in the museum. It meant: *Pay attention.* It meant: *Look here.*

He did. She was beautiful.

"Not as cool a uniform as yours," Amber replied, and there it was, the opening, the faintest flutter of something behind her eyes, her lips—but Elliot missed it, because he was looking down at himself. *His* uniform: he'd forgotten that he'd had it on, a baby-blue flight suit from the third Space Shuttle mission. In one pocket, Elliot had found a lighter; in another, a memo, in fading purple ink, forbidding lighters. "I can't believe they let you wear it," she said.

They didn't. But the museum—the eighth building in the entire country that Thomas Edison had wired, or so asserted a display case next to the adhesives—was undergoing a massive electrical upgrade, and its automatic security systems had been turned off. Indeed, the live-in blogger program was a secret way of supplementing the museum's human security force. The marketing director who'd explained this to Elliot thought it extremely clever, but ordered him not to write about it—*You wouldn't want to put your own security at risk*—and so Elliot rebelled in other ways, this way, wandering the museum at night, undressing mannequins, trying on their clothes. He'd come to find that the astronauts' outfits, while small (few knew how much the space program relied on short people), were the most comfortable.

"It's for the party," he said. "I'm supposed to make an appearance later, talk up the space program."

He wasn't.

But this much was true: Elliot was not unattractive. His ex-fiancée had told him that, and so had, begrudgingly, her mother. And he'd lost weight in the sphere, grown his hair long. Was—could—Amber be attracted to him? An experiment was called for.

"Follow me?" he said.

Thirty-seven days, and the only other woman he'd spoken to after hours had been Marie Curie, and she didn't count, since you knew what she was going to say depending on which button you pushed. *Be less curious about people and more curious about ideas.* She had a mannequin's body and a flat oval head, upon which flickered the projection of an actress's concerned face whenever the exhibit detected someone was near. *Watch out—radioactive experiment in progress!*

Amber looked away again. The party sounded centuries

distant.

So, too, was Elliot's old life. Twenty-two years old, twelve months out of a small Catholic college he had entered thinking he would become a priest and had left engaged to a woman who just eleven months ago had left him, Elliot was relearning how to relate to the world, to women. He was doing so scientifically, a word he preferred to *tentatively*.

Sometimes when the male lion is seeking a mate, he stands and walks out of the pride for some distance. He does not turn around during this walk; he stops at 100 yards and waits for one of the female lions to accept his invitation.

. Elliot had put those sentences in the blog last week, explaining that he had copied the passage from a poster in the Africa Annex, though he hadn't, he'd made it up, he was waiting to be caught.

As now. He'd let his last words to Amber hang in the air like his sphere, and walked away to see if she'd follow. It was hard to walk fast in the suit, but that was good—it would give her time to catch him.

Except she hadn't, and here he was, about to put his hand to the secret door.

He couldn't figure out how to pause without seeming to pause, so he went in. Who didn't follow an astronaut? Perhaps he should have dressed as Lincoln. Or Tesla.

The secret door led—initially—to a handicapped bathroom. The bathroom: it was all that museum visitors asked him about all day long. Sex: it was all that visitors to the museum's blog asked him about all night long. The bathroom answer was easy, was yes, they had it figured out; the sex answer was no, as in, no, they hadn't figured *that* out. Nor, to some degree, had Elliot. Not how to meet a woman, talk to her, kiss her, hold and be held, never fail or falter. College hadn't taught him. The museum hadn't taught him. Only this: that when the queen bee is ready to mate, she makes her way out of the hive, up through the sticky tube to the roof of the museum, and then up, up, up into the sky. The drones, the males, all pour out of the hive to chase her. She is stronger, twice their size, and keeps climbing. The ranks of suitors winnow as the exhausted fall away. Finally, only the strongest, bravest, finest male is left, and they mate. His sexual organ is of a piece with the rest of his insides; when he pulls away, she does not let go, and he falls to the earth, disemboweled.

Elliot thought some—many—of the museum's exhibits would

be better off without any explanatory signage whatsoever.

After a long minute, a cautious knock. It couldn't be Amber; the knock was too quiet and soft. So it had to be one of the guards, scared. Elliot had been surprised to discover how frightened the guards were, to a man, of the museum at night. *We see things on the monitors,* they said.

Once, one said, *I saw an astronaut visit the Plains Indian encampment and steal a baby.*

Elliot had put the baby right back. It had frightened him how light it was, how unclear it was that the baby was a just a doll. Its face, its eyes—

There had been a plastic baggie beneath the baby and he'd taken that instead. He kept it in here, behind the mirror. He wasn't sure what it was, though he had a hunch. And a hunch about Amber. He took the baggie out from its hiding place.

A second knock, louder now. He opened the door.

"*This* is the secret—" she said, but he interrupted her.

"No, this is—" he said, and she interrupted him.

"An interactive exhibit?" She pointed to the baggie. "Because, hello. Is that what I think it is?"

"Yes," Elliot answered, not because he knew, but because he'd thought, like she did, that it was pot. It was why he'd taken it. It was why, or partly why, his fiancée had left him. One critical night that he hadn't known was critical, he'd gone to that dark corner of the neighboring college's student union, where everyone knew you went to buy. But his fiancée had always been the one to go before, and that night, Elliot looked around and didn't know which guy with the backpack was the right guy, and everyone was looking at him oddly, intently, and he left. His fiancée had called him chicken and worse and she was right. And then she was gone. *Not because of that, just that, but because there's a lot you don't know about the world.* And that included what it was like to smoke pot. He'd been on a path to the priesthood. He hadn't had sex until he'd had it with her. He hadn't had wine until his parish started offering it at mass. He'd never stayed awake late enough to see *Saturday Night Live* live. And he'd never proposed to anyone until her parents said he had to.

Amber ducked inside. The door clicked shut. She was close enough now that he could smell her shampoo, see the spot on her neck where the wool uniform's high collar chafed, feel the heat coming off her.

She took the baggie. "This is ancient," she said with a quick, curious laugh. "You got robbed."

"I didn't pay for it."

"Good thing." She squeezed the bag together between her fingers and ground some of what was inside to dust, and Elliot felt his heart sink the way it had when he'd split the crotch of Abraham Lincoln's mannequin's pants. There was no going back now. "For both of us, I mean," she said. "I'm already flying. The brownies my brother sent were twice as strong as I thought they'd be. It's why I was exploring. I needed a place to come down."

"Like I said, I know just the spot. A hidden exhibit." He started to reach around her.

"Whoa, John Glenn," she said.

"I'm sorry, I just—" He didn't know what to say or do. Tesla, the coil, the sphere, the solitude. He wasn't well. Not entirely. But there was a way—just through here—

She frowned and then moved, which let him open a tiny door she hadn't seen. He ducked through and turned back for her.

"'One small step for a man . . .'" he said.

"Seriously?" she asked, her face bending down to his, close enough to kiss.

In the rear of the Hall of Flight was a poorly lit display of a memo William Safire provided Nixon forty-eight hours after Neil Armstrong's *Apollo 11* left earth, to be used as soon as it was confirmed there was no hope of return. Titled "In the Event of Moon Disaster," it prescribed words—*Fate has ordained that the men who went to the moon to explore in peace will stay on the moon to rest in peace*—and protocol. First, contact the "widows-to-be" by phone. Then, read statement on television. Then, have NASA cut communications with the lunar module. And finally, a "clergyman should adopt the same procedure as a burial at sea."

"Seriously," Elliot said.

A cramped passageway led to a ladder that led to a catwalk that led to the ceiling of the Hall of Flight. Decades ago, Edison, showing off, had wired the ceiling with hundreds of bulbs. From the catwalk above, the tracks of wires resembled a grim model-railroad display; from the floor beneath, where the partygoers were still mingling, it looked like what it was supposed to: the principal constellations of the Northern and Southern Hemispheres.

"There's even better," he said and led her on to a far part of the catwalk.

The zeppelin exhibit had been closed for years. Or rather, just this part. The zeppelin gondola itself was still visible from the floor below, suspended as it was from the ceiling, along with all the other historic aircraft. But invisible was this small access platform above. A series of panels discussed the history of zeppelins, the tragic polar flight of the airship *Italia*, the superior lift of hydrogen versus helium, the ability of some airships to receive, stow, and launch small airplanes, and the ease with which zeppelins once circumnavigated the globe.

"Look at this," Amber said. "A glass zeppelin ashtray, for people to use *onboard*, with a giant bag of *Hindenburg*-quality hydrogen two feet above their heads."

"Read carefully." He found himself whispering and so drew close. "It's an Esso ashtray. 'Esso,' S, O, Standard Oil. The glass isn't brown. It's filled with gasoline."

"Holy shit," she said and turned to him.

Somewhere, his fiancée had told him, *there is a museum of cowardice, and you are exhibit A.* She was keeping the ring, for example, because she knew he would let her. And she was getting rid of the baby, because she knew he would let her do that, too, and the ring would pay for it and a plane ticket besides, so she could fly far, far away—from her parents, from him.

And he'd said nothing.

And she'd said, *See?*

And he'd looked but he hadn't seen anything, not until now. Not until the gondola creaked slightly beneath their combined weight as he and Amber boarded, not until they felt their way to the zeppelin's back stateroom, not until he discovered that Amber's skin, vast and bright as it was upon discovery, with a spread of tiny moles across her stomach forming their own converse constellation, wasn't quite luminous enough for him to read her face, nor her his.

So he fumbled in the pockets of his discarded uniform for the lighter. Engraved, it said it had orbited the earth multiple times. Equally impressive would be if it still worked.

For a full ten minutes, there was nothing, nothing but a party coming to a close in the hall below and a wick lantern dangling romantically in the zeppelin above. In time, of course, the rain began, and for a long minute, the party guests really did think that it was rain, that the aging museum had one or two last tricks up its sleeve and one of them was weather, because how much harder could it be to have water fall from the ceiling if Tesla had bottled lightning, and Edison hardwired stars? But the tablecloths were white and the rain was red, or red-orange, from the rust of the sprinkler system, and people began to run.

Not everyone. Not Madame Curie; not the bees; not the space rock that, the hazmat team later determined, really should not have gotten wet; not the Plains Indians, who wondered if miracles might come in threes (their baby returned, rain erasing a century of dust—would the museum walls now fall away?); and not the unclothed couple in the first-class stateroom replica of the *D-LZ 127 Graf Zeppelin,* the first aircraft to fly over one million miles.

The Tesla coil shorted out. Elliot's blogosphere sheeted sprinkler spray like an underwater comet. The stateroom's curtains, rayon—once called "mother-in-law's silk," or so said the Hall of Wonders—which had caught fire when ass accidentally knocked lantern, were quickly saved by the water sluicing from the ceiling, but at the expense of the museum, whose glass disc sprinkler system, state of the art for 1890, would take the fire department hours to figure out how to shut off.

By then, of course, the two were gone, their uniforms, names, and identities, too, and years later, on the annual summer sojourn, not even their grandchildren knew the scuffed lighter by the cabin fireplace had such history, only that late at night, the grown-ups asleep, jarred lightning bugs forgotten, and the rest of the surrounding wilderness held at bay by the door, the flint spat spark after spark after spark, each a bright, brief universe, each an invitation to try again.

LISTEN

MY FATHER SPENT A GOOD PORTION OF HIS CAREER WITH A TAPE DECK slung over his shoulder, a slender, stubby microphone nosing into his pocket like a dog looking for a treat. Walking along, driving along, there was no telling when he'd stop, look up (not at anything specific), slowly turn the microphone on and press record. Horns, airplanes, footsteps, tires beating through wet leaves, the breathing of someone hiking in snow, trombone lessons from a block away, a hot air balloon when the flame is first lit. And voices: one, two, male, female, three on a street corner, twenty in a small room, hundreds in a theater. And crying and laughing and cursing and shouting, and screams. My father was really good at screams.

It was a good thing to be good at. Footsteps in snow might come and go, but there was a steady market for screams. You're shooting a war film, a horror film, a romantic film. There's a plane crash, a bomb explodes, someone jumps out of a cake. In the background, you hear a scream—or screams, if the director's a big spender. Those aren't always the screams of actors. Do you know what it costs to have an actor make a sound? Extras are so much cheaper when they're silent. No, those screams in the background—and sometimes, even the screams seemingly coming out of a star's mouth—those screams were often my father's doing. He collected, marketed, and rented them, singly and by the dozen, for decades. Just last year he sold his archive to a competitor, and though my father complained the lump sum was hardly equal to the years of future royalties he was giving up, he made out just fine. In fact, the amount he got was surprisingly large, given that a lot of his screams had aged. It wasn't that the sound quality was poor, but that the discerning ear could tell they were of a different era. Smokers, for example. There's not as much call for a smoker's scream as there once was. Or a man with a hat. My father always insisted a man with a hat screamed differently than a fellow without, but that was my father.

He tried to demonstrate once when I was home from college. He gave a little scream—a yelp, really—and told me to pay attention. He picked up a hat from the closet, an old fedora I'd never seen him wear. He put it on and yelped again.

"See?" he said, though he was asking if I'd heard.

"No," I said. "Sounds the same."

He took off the hat, yelped again, put it back on, yelped once more. "See?" My father's demeanor always veered between mad scientist and elementary school teacher, frenzied genius alternating with patronizing patience.

I shook my head again. I'd long learned the best way to annoy my father was to limit myself to soundless gestures.

"Well," he said, upset. He took the hat off and on, yelping all the while, more to himself as he went on. Finally, it came to him: "No, of course it doesn't sound different. *I* don't sound like a man with a hat screaming, because I don't wear hats. Doesn't matter if I just stick one on. Still sound like a bareheaded man." He went to put the hat away.

"Did my mother wear a hat?" I said.

"No." He didn't turn around.

"Do you think her scream would sound differently if she had?" I asked.

Now he turned. "No," he said quietly, balancing the brim of the hat in his hands.

I never knew my mother. I don't even remember the day my father told me that she had died, long ago. Her absence simply was, and always had been. Did I miss her? I suppose. In a way, I didn't know what a mother was, not really. I knew other kids had one, but I didn't.

I never knew my mother, but one strange night before leaving for college, I came to know her scream. And then the world did. It was an unusual sequence of events, but my mother's scream was unusual for many reasons, the biggest being that, late in his career, it became my father's biggest seller. It wasn't a classic scream; it didn't start with that aural punch, hold the note, and finally fade like a train heading off a bridge. No, hers came in three syllables: *ha-HA-huh.* There's no way you're going to figure out what it sounds like, but make the *A* sound like the one in *hat*, not *paw*, bite the last piece off too soon, make it the least bit musical, a little breathless, like you've been socked, and be thinking that the next sound out of your mouth is going to be a laugh.

Exactly. It makes no sense, especially the laugh, but trust me, it's all there. I've heard it a hundred, maybe a thousand times. It's called the Brenda, by the way, not my mother's name, not anyone's, far as I know. There were years when I'd hear it pop up in a film and I'd nudge my date and tell her about it later, but the results were always disastrous. I was slow to realize that admitting I was related to that scream was like admitting I was related to someone who'd been executed, something horrific that became unspeakable as soon as it became personal.

Because it was a horrible scream. It was short, but it was scary—and the hint of a laugh made it even scarier. You'd imagine it would get lost in the background, but it never did. You're thinking it's just because I knew it that I always heard it, but you could have asked anyone who was in the theater on a night my mother screamed. You left a little shaken, even if you didn't know why. It was a background scream, but it was better as a background scream. Front and center, it was too much; I've seen it dubbed into one or two actresses' mouths and it is awful—disturbing *and* unbelievable. Better to have it happen offstage, in the distance, a sound you sometimes didn't know you were hearing, a sound you never really heard until you yourself were walking alone one night down some dark, wet, deserted street, when suddenly the streetlight shudders out, and from a hidden doorway, moving as fast as if he's falling—

Did you gasp? Just a little? Good. That sound? That's part of it.

People paid my father for his screams, and he, in turn, paid people (much less) for theirs. In his early years, he relied mostly on drama students from NYU or some of the private acting schools around Manhattan. Students would scream until they were hoarse, again and again, as my father pressed them for something they could never quite give him—"an ounce of real" is what he called it. The closest he ever came with a student was when she screamed at him on the way out. He'd given her ten dollars for a half hour of operatic shrieking, and she was almost in tears.

Not because of the money, nor because her voice was almost gone, but because of the noise, the noise, the *noise*. She felt as if she were going mad, and she screamed. As the door to the studio shut soundlessly behind her, my father raced back to see if the tape was still rolling. It was. He ran after her with another five dollars, but she wouldn't take it. She screamed again ("Not as good, if you want to know the truth," my father later observed) and fled. Her scream became the Sally, and my father made decent money off it. It was a solid, workhorse scream, the kind you reach for when the person is offscreen getting murdered, and shouts less from fear than fury.

It was after her that my father turned to "civilians," as he called them, for his screams. Now, he didn't do "live" screams; that is, he never recorded someone who was actually in trouble. You couldn't count on that kind of luck anyway. No, he'd put an ad in the paper—something like *I'll pay to hear your voice!* plus a time and an address—and wait to see who showed. He toyed with ideas of how he would get good screams out of people—should he scare them somehow? Show them horrible pictures? Movie clips?

But the truth is my father didn't have it in him to scare people. He was always *listening* for a new sound, and when he wasn't listening, he was taping. The result was that he spoke, and emoted, very little. Like every boy, I have a Little League story. Except mine isn't of a father yelling, or even getting in the way of the action with his camera. When I rounded third after my home run, I saw my father in the stands, absolutely still, his back to me, his hand holding a microphone to the crowd.

So when those first civilians showed up for taping, my father did nothing more than simply ask them to scream. Among the ones who stayed, a pattern emerged. First scream, they giggled, second scream, their voice gave out too soon—takes a greater amount of air than you think—and the third scream? You started making money as soon as they opened their mouths. Fourth, fifth, sixth scream, until they couldn't go on: the worst of the lot was ten times better than the best drama student.

My father had theories. At a certain point, he thought, the brain stops second-guessing what's being asked of the vocal cords: if I'm screaming, there must be a reason, the mind figures, and the person just surrenders to it. Now a good actor, a great actor, might be able to will such emotion into being. But for variety, and price, you couldn't beat the strangers my father found. Their screams became the Tommy, the Bertie, the Carol, the Betty-Ann—hell, Lou, Francis, Frances, Johnny, Cindy, Todd, the Mr. Tambs, and Hazel—sweet Jesus, I hope I never hear another Hazel. There were dozens. I once asked him where he got the names, and why he used the names of people: why not use numbers?

"Would you buy a Corvette if it was named the 84-79-08?" he asked, shaking his head.

I was only nine at the time. Too young to buy a Corvette, and too young to know that my father was shaking his head not because I'd asked the question but because he thought I was the type who would, in fact, buy a car that had a number for a name. (And I did, as it happens, a Mazda 626, but that does not prove my father's point.)

I'd say a third to half of my childhood conversations with my father ended this way, with him shaking his head and looking at me sadly. Another variation: him shaking his head and saying, "You sound just like your mother, God rest her soul." It was in this way that my mother lived with us, through these apologetic benedictions, through photographs, and, of course, on tape.

Not her scream, not that tape, not yet. Just the tapes of everyday sound, of her, of them, at home doing whatever they did before I came along.

Sometimes, it seemed like he'd left the tape recorder on for an entire afternoon or evening. You could hear a vacuum going, or birds outside singing, maybe a radio in another room, the clatter of dishes in the kitchen. Then, steps.

"That's your mother," my father would always say. I would sometimes want to ask a question, but he would shush me, and close his eyes. He always considered listening, even at the movies, to be too important a task to let vision distract.

So I would close my eyes, too. They had lived where we lived, in an old row house, a wonderful place for sound. Hardwood floors throughout. Steam heat. Rickety stairs. And out back, on the other side of the alley, a Chinese cemetery that every animal on the island visited each night, yipping and snarling while they devoured the meals people left for deceased relatives.

Stairs, steam, animals keening in cemeteries: to think about it now, it's amazing that I could have heard my mother at all above the din. But there she was, walking to and fro across the invisible room, before an invisible microphone, placed there by my invisible father. Step, step, step, step. God, those steps, that sound! That *is* childhood to me, the way others hold as their touchstones the color of the ocean in a particular picture book, the smell of a Christmas tree, the taste of sunflower seeds or salt from the sea.

Those tapes, like the fact of my mother's death, always were. I don't remember when my father started playing them, how he first introduced them, how I first reacted.

I do remember when he stopped playing them for me. I was

fourteen and had a friend over. I had told him about the tapes and he wanted to hear them. I wanted him to hear them, too.

My father was horrified. My friend didn't know that, but I knew the various grades of my father's silences, and I knew he was displeased. It wasn't until later that evening after the shrugging friend had wandered home alone that my father sat me down and explained: We could never play the tapes for anyone, not friends, not even family (and we had little that passed for family—an aunt on my father's side, who sent unsigned Christmas cards, no one on my mother's side). They were private. Moreover, people wouldn't understand.

I didn't realize it until right at that moment, and maybe not fully until years later: Of course they wouldn't understand. A widower and his only son, listening to tapes of the departed wife and mother? But what really pained him—this is what took me a little longer to realize—was that the tapes themselves were odd. Because for all the normal household noise my mother made, she never spoke.

Not a word. Sometimes, when she was in the kitchen (you could triangulate locations by sound: dishes + water + faraway footsteps), you could hear humming, but only very faintly. And occasionally, a voice, but that would turn out to be a scrap of a radio program that she was listening to.

Like I said, this didn't seem odd to me until my father suggested that other people wouldn't understand. It wasn't that I'd never wondered about this before—but then, the answer seemed obvious: My mother never spoke because my father was taping. He was a sound engineer, after all. She wasn't about to spoil his tape. When he left that tape recording going for hours at a stretch at home, he was trying to collect the background sounds of a house, he once explained. You couldn't have people speaking in that background, because that would make the tape less attractive to a movie director. Footsteps were fine. Anonymous, for the most part. But if a director wanted voices, he'd prefer to add them himself—men, women, kids, his top-billed star, or some character actor. He didn't want to have my father's wife in the background chattering. Or screaming.

Blurry photographs. Muffled tapes. Believe it or not—and thinking back, I sometimes don't—it took me until I was through high school to decide that my father was making my mother up, that the image, indistinct though it was, was as complete a fiction as the movies my father contributed to.

But why? That's almost too big a question for me now; it certainly was too much for me at the time. It was bad enough to be missing a mother, bad enough to have a father whose own reserve exacerbated her absence, but also to be the victim of a grotesque hoax? It was beyond consideration. But I had to know—or, I had to let him know what I didn't know, which I did, not by confronting him directly (I wasn't that brave, and I wasn't that sure I wanted to know the truth) but by picking at him with question after question. Why did he have only her footsteps, not her voice on tape? Why didn't we have more photographs? Why did the ones we did have all look so indistinct, so different? Where was mom buried? Why didn't we visit?

Why wasn't there anyone else I could ask these questions of?

I'd come to my own conclusion, a romantic one, which was that I was adopted, that my father had no idea who my mother was, that my father, a single man, had adopted me because he was lonely, only to realize his loneliness was indelible and only deepened by his adopting an orphan.

No wonder he specialized in screams.

My father parried these questions as he had done for years, with much the same answers he'd always given, though I was gratified to see my renewed, vindictive teenaged persistence winnow away his humor and patience. We both knew that he would crack, soon. I assumed that he'd tell me before I left for college, for good, and this turned out to be correct.

It was my last night at home. We'd gone out to dinner, an uncharacteristic event, and he'd had three glasses of wine, also uncharacteristic (but promising, I thought). When we returned home, he got out the tape deck and set it up at the little dining room table, the microphone aimed at me. Then, to my weary dismay, he went to fetch the "memory master." This was a reel onto which my father had dubbed my life up until that point—my early babblings, toddler rantings, a snippet or two of a spelling bee I'd lost, the crowd after that home run, my name announced at graduation. This was also the reel on which were preserved some of my "mother's" ghostly footsteps and the rest of her silent life. I'd long before come to think the tape extremely corny, but my father placed a great value on it, keeping it under lock and key, which I cynically assumed was meant to impress me, though it no longer did.

Once he'd threaded the tape through the reel and cued it—the ceremony mattered to him; he would never have survived in this digital world, where recording can begin with nothing other than a finger's soundless tap—he told me to say a few things about what was going on, how I felt about going to college, what I was hoping to do, what I was going to do after I graduated. I complied as listlessly as I could.

Maybe it was my disregard for the occasion, maybe it was the niggling assault I'd previously subjected him to, maybe it was the wine— or maybe it was something he'd planned all along. But after I finished, he pressed stop and looked at the machine.

"You've been asking about your mother a lot."

Here was the moment at last, and I could say nothing. "You— you don't believe what you've heard," he went on, an awkward way to put it, perhaps, but not so to a man of sound.

"There's—there's something I've never played for you," he said now, rewinding the tape. "It's—well, it's just—there's no real way to introduce this." He fell silent as we both watched the tape diminish on one reel and grow on the other. Finally, the tape ran clear; we'd reached the lead, and he hit stop.

"This is your mother." He pressed play.

My mother was crying. And because I was a professional's son, my first thought was that she was doing an awful job of it, snorkeling her way through a kind of oily blubbering. I looked over and saw my father crying, inaudibly, which made me tear up, and then grow angry. Angry at my mother for making my father cry, angry with myself for doubting him all this time. Because this was not an ounce of reality, but the full weight of it: this was no actress, no stranger, but my mother. The crying was that off-key, that intimate, that consuming. It was a tiny sound, but it filled the room, and it was time, past time, to turn it off. He was shaking his head now; I reached out to press "stop."

Then came the scream.

It was my mother's scream, the whole, eerie, penetrating tear of it, anguished and exhausted and even foolish, and then it was quiet. Not blank tape, just taped silence. My father looked up, drew a breath, and I stopped the tape.

He stared at the tape machine for a minute, a full and quiet minute, and during that time I stared at him. He was white, and sweating, and for the first time, I realized he was old.

"Your mother—" he started to say, but I cut him off.

"I'm sorry," I said. "I'm sorry I kept asking."

He looked at me with mild surprise, and exhaled, soft and low and controlled.

"Why—why was she crying?" I asked. "And what was that scream?"

He shook his head, slowly—at me, or at her memory, I wasn't sure—and began, "When I met your mother, she was just starting out, an actress."

And he didn't need to say another word. That is, he was ready to, but I didn't want him to; I didn't want to hear another sound. Not from him, not from the tape, not from my mother. Because I could see what had happened. He'd had her into the studio, he'd had her cry, scream. They'd fallen in love—maybe that was the source of that almost-laugh at the end of the scream, maybe they were already falling in love, right at that very moment, astounded at the ridiculous circumstances.

And then what? Then me, of course, but after that, she died? How? When? At that instant, I did not want to know. This was a perfect moment, and all I wanted to do—all I knew how to do—was to extend it, make it last. Another word from my dad, another sound, would ruin it. So with a grace and calm that I thought extremely mature at the time but now find distinctly childlike, I silently led my father from the room. He seemed a bit dumbfounded, but also grateful. I went straight to bed. I didn't sleep, of course, and didn't plan to, but must have closed my eyes near dawn and opened them not long after, when the morning calls of the birds outside entered my dreams. Their voices briefly became my mother's, which was enough to wrench me awake.

My father was not a whistler (on principle; he thought it the essence of audio amateurism), but if he had been, he would have been that morning. He greeted me with a full breakfast, delighted in making a small ritual of serving me my first cup of coffee—"Welcome to adulthood!"—and nattered away about preparations for my trip.

I thought it was his way of avoiding talking about the night before, but he brought it up himself once we were in the car on the way to the train. He hadn't had a chance to tell me about the circumstances of the tape, he explained, and was worried that I would worry—which I should not. I should understand: my mother was an actress, but they'd met outside the studio, and he'd been happy to keep her outside the studio. He thought there'd be no way he'd get a useful scream out of someone he knew so well, even if she was a professional.

This rankled her, of course, and that's why she went ahead and made her own tape. Gave it to him one day when he came home, a kind of audition. She wanted to be one of his sounds; she was jealous that he recorded perfect strangers and that they were the ones who ended up in the movies, while she seemed to be trapped doing shows farther and farther off-Broadway.

The tape, of course, was awful. Poignant, and cute, perhaps—but that was why it was awful. They'd had a laugh about it, because the whole thing was a lark. (And that's how it sounded. That strange smile at the end of the scream was evidence enough, a wink between two lovers.)

He drew a deep breath. We'd reached the station and parked. He was still staring out the window, hands on the wheel. He never played the tape, he said, because it made him too sad. The fake tears, the giggle-scream. He should have played it for me earlier, he said, and apologized. It was just that he'd been waiting. Because to understand it, to understand the whole crazy thing, I had to be old enough. But now, now that he'd played it, maybe he'd do something with it. He'd always meant to do something with the tape, some kind of private memorial to her, but that was foolish, he knew. The crying and the scream were just so plain bad, for one.

"They're not that bad," I broke in. "The crying is—well, the crying is bad." My father winced, and I waited before going on. What was I going to say? I didn't really know how to speak to my father about my mother, about love, about anything. But technique, the business of sound: I became aware that could be—always had been—a refuge, a place for us to meet, and my relief was so profound it was audible.

"She sounds like a fat man crying." I laughed a professional little laugh. "But the scream—is really different. Unique. I bet you could do something with it." The challenge now was how to use such shoptalk to help my father out of (or into) his emotional well. He seemed to know I was attempting some sort of verbal sleight of hand and looked at me, both afraid and eager. So I went on. "Wouldn't *that* be a better memorial," I asked, "to get her, finally, in the movies, where she wanted to be?" My father's eyes glazed with tears; he started to smile. When it finally came time to run for the train, he pulled me back in a kind of clutch, or hug.

An irony of my exposure to my father's work is that "real" screams always sound artificial to me. I was once at a hockey game, right down next to the ice, when a player suffered a tendon torn in two. There could not have been anything more authentic than his screaming, and the crowd went silent before it. But all I could hear was its imperfections—he wasn't taking big enough breaths, the scream was petering out too quickly, the tone was too unsteady. Nothing wrong with an unusual scream (my mother's was proof of that), but the hockey player sounded like an amateur.

So, too, my father, the last time I saw him. Actually, I heard him before I saw him. I was outside the door, getting briefed by a nurse. "It's not too late," the nurse was saying, and thereupon came, from inside a room nearby, this strange noise—soft, high, thin, weak. Unignorable, unnamable.

"So much has fallen so silent," my father despaired at his retirement. Take offices. Take almost anything. Typewriters made music;

typing on a touchscreen makes no noise at all (and today's devices muffle music inside *earbuds,* a word he despised). And screams. Once upon a time, my father said, you could find within a scream the DNA of that world's entire moment—its fears and ambitions and its strangely exuberant, apparently widespread belief that if you raised your voice high enough, you'd be heard.

The sound came again as I entered the room, and now I could see it, a hiss, a hum, something sharp freed from something deeper; it had shape and color and volume, everything his own face and form and mouth no longer had.

"Dad," I said. His eyes were closed. Machines all around sucked and beeped and clicked. "Can you hear me?"

CALLED

JESUS CALLED ALL THE TIME WHEN WE LIVED ON KENSINGTON ROAD. The cordless phone and only the cordless phone would ring once and only once, and if you picked it up, as we almost never did, no one would be there.

When our son was old enough to ask about this phenomenon, my wife, having spent her sanity on three dozen other questions from him earlier that day, simply said, "It's Jesus calling." And because my son, who never let an answer pass without a question, accepted this one without so much as a peep, the matter stood. Jesus called.

Someone told us the phone's problems had something to do with baby monitors, which we didn't have, or voice mail, which we did. Something in the line would cause the phone to warble once and that was that. The truth was, the phone was cheap; I'd bought it at the supermarket, which, as my wife often reminded me, should have been some sort of clue. Or sign, given that she'd pinned Jesus on the matter.

I once heard Harry explaining in earnest to one of his little friends that Jesus called our house occasionally. I broke into the conversation quickly with a clumsy redirect: "Not Jesus, Harry. Jésus. *Hay-zoose.*" I looked carefully at his friend, partly to make sure this sank in, and partly because I couldn't bear to look at Harry. "Our good friend *Hay-zoose,*" I smiled. "Olé!" I tagged on out of foolishness. This only led to further confusion as Harry started referring to Jesus as *Hay-zoose* at vacation Bible camp, but we were spared any additional grief.

When Harry grew older, we gently disabused him of any misconceptions about the phone, of which, it turned out, he had many. His child's imagination had taken Jesus's one ring and had embroidered a rather vast telecommunications-based theology—including the impact of call-waiting on prayers and the significance of Superman changing in phone booths. Nevertheless, Harry ultimately accepted our explanation. He was a little disappointed, but such are the disappointments of childhood (although we let him have a couple additional years with Santa Claus).

When we moved, our new house must have been bewitched by different forces or lain in a gully of spiritual calm, because very little out of the ordinary happened there. Certainly, Jesus never called again. It may have been out of pique; I had purchased a new phone by that point—at an electronics store, to appease my wife, although I was hardly certain a store that specialized in stereos would know anything more about phones than one that specialized in groceries—and the cordless phone was relegated to the closet.

It came out again when Harry was waist deep in high school, and what phones we had—this being long before cell phones—rang off the hook with news of tests and games and dates and concerts and God knows what else. He wanted a phone in his room, but we parents had no interest. It was not so much the expense but the independence, the autonomy, the budding adulthood that troubled us. So he dusted off the old cordless, plugged it in down the hall, and toted the handset back into his room whenever his discussions warranted such discretion, which was apparently often.

We thought he would give up this ruse fairly soon—even when Jesus called, the phone never worked very well. It often sounded as though you were calling from lunar orbit in the midst of a solar storm, and occasionally the phone went dead after just a few minutes of use, which my wife, again, averred was less a failure of the phone than a feature, designed to remind you that you had, after all, bought the flimsy phone at a *supermarket*—and come to think of it, weren't you running low on milk?

But Harry persevered; he and the phone disappeared behind his closed door for hours at a stretch, with the little red "in use" light glowing smugly from the base unit down the hall whenever we passed by. Among the limited features of the base unit was a "page" button; if you pressed this, the handset would beep, allowing you to seek it out in whatever far corner of the house you had mislaid it. We had often used it to remind ourselves of our growing blindness; pressing the page button often revealed the phone to be an arm's length away.

This day, Harry had been "in use" for quite some time, and I was heading down to his room to knock on the door and get him to hang up. I regarded parents who simply picked up another extension and told their teen to get off the line as rather uncouth; why announce to the world that you have no control over the communications in your own home? No, our solution—knocking—was quite civilized and, I imagined, better received by Harry. But passing the base unit, something about that bright-red glowing eye glowering at me got my dander up, and I pressed the page button.

The door to his room sprang open, and he greeted me with a face contorted in alarm, his face as red as his hair. He looked at me as though someone had just broken into the house and I was refusing to do anything about it, and his glare managed to make me feel like both foiled burglar and failed watchman.

"Dad!" he all but cried.

"I'm—sorry." I tried to recover quickly. "I needed the phone. I didn't even know that old button worked."

"Dad!" he repeated, and I watched him carefully, because I knew somehow that I was watching the end of something. Some parents see it when their child waves good-bye that first day of school, others the first time he pulls away from the curb in the car alone, others when he walks down the aisle. For me, it was there, in the hallway, with my son holding the phone from the supermarket, which Jesus used to ring, and who, as I would learn in a moment, was now on the line.

"I'm on the *phone*," Harry said, though he did not hurry back to his call.

"Well, I'm sorry, but you've been *on* the phone, and now you need to be *off*."

"I'm on the phone with Jesus," Harry said, frowning to himself.

"Well, tell *Hay-zoos* your *padre* needs to use *el teléfono*."

Harry gave me a little disappointed smile that aged and distanced me thirty years and left me with no doubt that Harry believed whoever on the line was Jesus more than he believed I was his father. I attempted retreat, but by then, it was too late: "Well, when you're off, just give a call—I mean, shout down. Oh, whatever, Harry. My best to"—I was going to make a joke, but caught myself—"him." I clomped back down the hall.

Of course I wanted to call my wife immediately. But she was out doing errands, and besides, Harry was on the phone. Instead, I practiced what I would say to her.

You'll never guess who Harry was on the phone with today . . .

Wait till you see our long-distance bill this month . . .

Know that little page button? Well, I . . .

If you hadn't had been so quick with the "Jesus" thing twelve years ago . . .

Your son has lost his marbles . . .

In the end, I used all the lines, out in the driveway before she could even get out of the car. It turned into a regular little spat. Maybe if I'd taken religion seriously, maybe if I'd played catch with him earlier, maybe if I just calmed down and stopped overreacting. Once done with me, she started in on herself, and by the end of the talk, we'd both decided that we were lousy, awful parents, but we'd had some good times along the way, hadn't we, and maybe the in-studio audience would look on us kindly when it got to that: "Parents whose children dial deities."

We ordered pizza, even though it was Saturday, which meant that we had time to cook. But Harry preferred pizza delivery to anything else, and $9.99 seemed such a cheap price to pay to win back your son's love and affection and forgiveness for your sins.

"Hey, Mom," Harry said pleasantly, walking into the kitchen. We'd just hung up with the pizza man and both of us wanted to blurt out the glorious news first.

"We—"

"Peetz—"

"I—"

Harry just looked us. "I'm sorry," I finally said. "Shouldn't have broken in." Harry gave that little disappointed smile again, but this time, he'd softened it into something that was still patronizing but affectionate.

"Hey, Dad, no problem. He said not to worry about it." Harry clapped a hand on my shoulder and I felt relief for a moment, and horror the next. "He" just had to be He. It fell to my wife to ask the question.

"Who were you on the phone with?" she asked Harry, matching pleasant for pleasant.

"Jesus," said Harry, with a confident, grateful nod. "Wow," he commented, shaking his head in recollection. "I mean, wow."

"Jesus?" said my wife.

"Not *Hay-zoose,*" I confirmed for her, and she shot me a little look. Harry rolled his eyes with sitcom timing and started rooting around in the fridge.

"The King of Kings," Harry said; I heard the clink of a bottle and had a flash of panic—beer—was he going to start drinking now, too? We'd had it so easy up until now, I realized. He emerged with the milk carton. I relaxed. At least Jesus wasn't a bad influence, not yet.

We all looked at each other for a long while, and Harry just stared on, pleased, and even proud. We didn't know him, I decided. Whatever molecules of ours that still floated around in him had lost their power to resonate, to echo back what inner mysteries his face wouldn't tell us.

My wife broke first. "Harry, what is this? What do you mean, Jesus? I mean, I know *who* you mean"—this, with a dark glance at me—"but who—who—who is on the phone? With you, I mean? Who's Jesus?"

"Well, the risen Lord, of course," Harry said matter-of-factly, "but you're asking more than that, aren't you? And to that, I really can't say—I don't know myself yet." He started to leave.

"Harry!" my wife called, which made me anxious but also proud: she was better than I at exacting discipline or, at least, at getting answers. "What are we up to here? Putting aside 'who' for a moment, let's do 'how.' How did this all come to be, this Jesus?"

"Well, the phone . . ." Harry started, showing the first signs of discomfort.

"Yes, the phone, Harry, we joked about that long ago. Your father bought that at the *supermarket*. God help us if Jesus has seized upon those phones to start chatting up earth, because I think most people threw them away." Another look at me. "As we should have. They were garbage." Harry looked hurt, but she could withstand it longer than I could. "Harry—I just want to know what's going on. You've never talked about this before. And you can stand there, smiling and sure, and tell us you've been talking to Jesus, but you can still recognize why this is wacko, can't you? Why poor imperfect parents like us might not get it?" She reached out for his hand, and I saw him flinch to pull it away, but he was still, at this point, too much her son. Instead, he bit his lip, which wasn't quite like pulling a knife on her but cut deeply all the same. "Honey," she said softly.

Harry looked at me, and then at his mother. "I love you, Mom." He looked at me again. "I'm sorry this upset you; I guess I thought you'd think it was kind of cool." He considered things. "But He said it would be hard at first. People, you know, wouldn't understand and stuff."

"He said that?" my wife asked.

"What else did he say?" I asked.

"Oh, lots of stuff."

"Like what?" I asked again, trying, and I think succeeding, to keep things pleasant, open.

"Lots of stuff, but He's not finished yet, and I don't want to get it all mixed up before I get it right," Harry said earnestly. "I've got to go back upstairs. He may call again."

"We're having pizza," I said, and nothing ever sounded so horrible to me. This was my trump card? Still, I could see the same hope rising in my wife's eyes as I knew rose in mine.

"Cool," Harry said. "Save some for me!" He strode out and up the stairs.

"He's tired," I said, when we heard the door to his room close.

"Please, he's not tired, I haven't seen him so awake since third grade," my wife answered. She tore the pizza coupon into little bits.

"Hey," I said, before catching myself, "we need that."

"Jesus, we need—there's that Jesus again. Jesus."

"Maybe—" I started.

"I have nothing against the man," she said absently, pulling out our phone books. "What do you think: Harry? Is he just crazy? Who's he talking to? Did you listen in?" I frowned. "I think you'd be forgiven in this case. I mean, Jesus. That's a rare treat."

"Careful now," I said.

"We go to church. We don't do crack. We love our son. We mow our lawn. We're decent parents." She'd meant this as a statement, but it came out a question, which I answered.

"Yes we are. This is not about us. This is about Harry."

"This *is* about us," she said. "When kids go shoot up schools, they don't blame the kids, or the guns; they go after the parents. Harry talking to Jesus is coming right back here." She pointed between her eyes.

"Harry's always been a little . . ." I drifted off, because I didn't know the word, there wasn't a word for it, but I knew she'd know what I meant.

"A little what?" she demanded.

"You know, a little—"

"Don't say different," she said, which I would have, even though I knew it was the wrong word, too.

"Thoughtful," I tried.

"Thoughtful?"

"Thoughtful. When you first told him it was Jesus on the line, he shut up; he didn't question it. Remember that, way back when? Some things he just takes in, turns them over. How many times have his teachers told us that? Once he gets a hold of something, he doesn't let go? He works it and works it . . ."

"Oh please, they were talking about his science project. Those damn birds. The first time they'd let a student continue his science project from one year to the next. He was so into it, I think they were afraid to make him drop it."

"Exactly—that's what he does—he gets completely engrossed in things. Obsessed."

"Where does he get that from?" she said. If this was directed at me, I was incredulous. Obsessiveness was not among my many faults and she knew this.

"Redheads," I joked. I mean, it was a joke—he got his hair from her—but she broke down crying.

"We're losing him, don't you see?" she said. "We're losing him to something—to someone else." At this she stiffened up and her eyes grew bright. "Some*one* else."

"Jesus," I said.

"Please! Someone else—he's talking to *someone* on that phone, right? Someone posing as Jesus."

I looked at her, but it wasn't enough. "No. Harry's a smart boy. He's not going to pick up the phone and think Jesus is there." But after I said it, I couldn't close my mouth.

"Someone's got him," my wife said. "Someone's got to him, somehow, somewhere, and convinced Harry that he's Jesus."

"Starting with us," I said. I had bought the phone. She had told Harry it was Jesus calling.

She shook her head. "Let's start with those experts down at the church. I bet they've seen this before with impressionable kids."

"Like Joan of Arc."

"Not helping," she said, picked up the phone, and cautiously held it to her ear. "Dial tone," she said, exhaling.

I went to the foot of the stairs and looked up. I could hear nothing, I could see nothing. The house was just as it was before, a quiet place on a quiet Saturday.

After paying full price for the pizza, I brought it into the kitchen and set it on the counter. My wife smiled wide when she saw me, but she kept talking to Father Castigliano, whom she had had on the phone now for the better part of an hour. I opened the box until she gestured frantically at me to leave it closed. I wandered back out to the stairs and called for Harry.

No door creaked, no reply.

I climbed up the stairs. Perhaps he couldn't hear me. Certainly he wasn't on with Jesus now that my wife was on the phone. I started down the hallway, avoiding at all costs the sight of the base unit, which I believed bore a large share of responsibility for all that had transpired. I got to Harry's door and knocked. "Pizza!" I shouted again and, again, was answered only with silence. Normally, I would have just opened the door, but I gave another shout—with a jovial air I initially thought came from some deep reserve inside me, but quickly realized I'd borrowed from the rotund cartoon chef on the lid of the pizza box. I retreated down the hallway, too wrapped up in wondering what Harry was up to now to avert my gaze when I came even with the base unit.

And there it was. Glowing at full, sickening strength, the little "in use" button. Harry was on the phone. We only had one line. My wife was on a corded phone. Harry was listening in. I looked down the hall; the door was still closed. I ran downstairs and rushed into the kitchen with eyes wide enough for my wife to put the good father on hold with the palm of her hand. "What?" she hissed.

"He's on the phone!"

"Jesus?"

"No, Harry, Harry, he's on the phone—he can *hear* you."

"Oh—well—fuck," my wife said. She uncupped the phone. "Father? Can I call you? Can I call you back? . . . Oh yes, no—that does sound like—listen, I need to hop off right now. I'm sorry—no—yes—thanks."

"Was it bad?" I said.

"No, it wasn't 'bad.'" She opened the pizza and studied it.

"What did he say?" I asked. "If Harry heard you talking about him—and if you and Father Castigliano said—"

"We said nothing. I hope Harry did hear. He'd hear his mother just about dying." The phone rang. Once. We looked at each other. It didn't ring again. I answered it. I heard nothing, but I didn't hear a dial tone, so I knew the line was open.

"Harry?" I asked. I thought I could hear breathing.

"Hello," came a voice, weak and tinny, muffled by the scratches and clicks of what sounded less like a bad connection than a very old recording.

"Hello?" I almost shouted, and my wife looked up at me, stunned.

"Do you hear me?" the voice came again, surfacing briefly from the murk.

"Who is this?" I shouted. "Harry!"

"I can hear you fine," said the voice.

"Harry!" I shouted again.

"That's good," the voice said soothingly, and the line went dead—no dial tone, no sound. I dropped the phone and ran for the stairs. My wife followed. I ran past the base unit, where the light still glowed and threw open the door to Harry's room, and was horrified, but not surprised, to find him gone.

As in gone. For a while, my wife and I started attending daily mass at 6 a.m. We went to confession. We prayed the rosary. The plan was, as my wife put it, to "smoke this Jesus out." If it really was Jesus—and this we had to consider, since no one else had emerged, and Harry was most definitely missing—maybe we'd find him on his own turf.

But six months of this produced nothing—no meetings with nor words from Jesus, and no sign of Harry. So we got angry, then sad, then angrier still, and then tired. We stayed tired. We stayed home. We turned off the ringers to all the phones (we'd never found the missing handset to the cordless phone) and let the answering machine take all the calls, always with an ear out in case it was Harry calling, telling us that he was fine, that it was all a dream, and that he'd be home soon. We believed this, but the police did not. The problem with runaways, they explained, is they want to stay lost. If they're not back on their own in six weeks, the police said, prepare for life without them. They didn't say it that bluntly, but they didn't have to. They had no leads.

Neither did Father Castigliano, who, upsettingly, always made a point of reminding us that it had to be some "mentally unwell" individual impersonating Jesus at the heart of this. We should not hold this against Father Castigliano. Nor Jesus. Father Castigliano included Harry in his prayers, he assured us, though he must have meant in private, as I never heard him do so publicly. Word had somehow leaked out—through the police, I imagine, though they denied this—

that our son's disappearance was tied to Jesus calling. And, of course,

Father Castigliano wanted to do all he could to distance himself and the

parish from such hysteria.

Plenty of others, however, rushed to fill the gap. We had some

initial interest from some "pilgrims," who'd been making the rounds of

Marian miracles—statues of the Virgin Mary weeping or bleeding or

her face appearing in the bark of a tree. But the advance scouts found

little of interest in our home, and even less in us. We didn't believe it had

really been Jesus on the phone who had called our son away, and if we

didn't believe, what kind of pilgrim hosts would we be?

We thought about moving. The house was closing in on us, and we

began to realize that we not only missed Harry, we envied him. He'd

left; he'd escaped. We were left behind, in a little silent prison formed

by the space his absence left and reinforced by the four walls that had

contained us all.

We cleaned out closets, divvied up piles for garbage and

Goodwill, and even went so far as to clean out the kitchen cabinets of almost all our food. But in the end, we couldn't move. There was always a chance Harry would come back—would at least call—and we wanted to be ready to receive him.

We had thrown or given away all of our food prior to our aborted move, as though we never planned to eat again, and so found ourselves quite hungry that first weekend in our new-old home. The thought of eating out yet again or ordering in sent nausea coursing through us, so we headed for the supermarket. Once there, we split up—we had never been good joint grocery-shoppers, my wife and I, and weren't good at doing much of anything together at that point. My wife took the basket and the list, while I browsed the end aisles for "boy bargains," my wife's term for sale items stacked at the end of an aisle that unattended husbands unfailingly picked up.

I came upon a Christmas-in-July display, which teetered with dusty Christmas relics that had failed to move—napkins, cups, tins of cookies, and largish plastic Santa figurines that turned out to be phones. I picked one up. I hadn't seen any phones in the supermarket since purchasing Jesus's phone, ages ago. I turned the package over to see if anything was recognizable, and indeed, the manufacturer was the same. I put it back on the display and looked at Santa for a while. If he winked, I decided, I would buy the phone. I had come to organize my life according to such supernatural bargains—if I go running ten days in a row, if I stop eating dessert, if the first car and last car I see tomorrow is blue, Harry will come home—and I stared hard. Santa stared back, plastic and pitiless. Then, without moving his lips, he spoke. "Ho, ho, ho!"

I gasped, not because he spoke, but because the voice was exactly the same one I'd heard on that call—that last call so many years ago: thin, tinny, distant, vacant. I looked around and leaned in, but there was nothing. I backed up a little to see if the Santa I was staring at was, in fact, the one making the noise.

"Ho, ho, ho," he said again, and I snatched him up. The one with the chipped nose. A package of napkins slid to the floor. "Ho, ho, ho," the Santa said again, softer now. And then, nothing. I prowled up and down the store, in search of my wife. She wasn't pleased when she saw me.

"No," she said.

"It's—" I said, barely able to contain myself. "The voice—it sounds like—maybe—?" She took it from me, looked Santa in the eye, looked me in the eye.

"Less than $5?" she said.

"Twelve," I answered. She tossed it in the basket. It looked fragile. She looked fragile. I did what I should not have, which was bring it home and set it up in Harry's room.

Soon after it was plugged in, the voice came again, "Ho, ho, ho," just as the other phones in the house began to ring. "Ho, ho, ho," it said again. My wife tried to pick up the receiver, but I batted her hand away. She ran from the room and snatched up another receiver. The ringing stopped. The ho-ho-hoing stopped. I heard my wife talking to her mother in a high tremolo and then hang up. Santa emitted another ho-ho-ho and was silent. I sat on the floor, staring at it.

I realized I didn't even know how the phone worked, and studied it for a second before I discovered that it functioned like an old-fashioned telephone. His head, with a cord dangling off his hood, was the earpiece. You picked it up, revealing a keypad, and spoke into Santa's stomach. I imagined it would easily terrify children. I listened through Santa's head for a voice, but heard only dial tone. I hung up when my wife came back in. She pulled me up from the floor; we went to bed and did not sleep.

"What if he does call?" my wife finally said.

"What do you mean?" I asked.

"What if he calls, what do we say?"

"We tell him we love him—"

"No," my wife broke in.

I continued. "We tell him to come home. We tell him we love him, loved him, come home, come home."

"No," my wife said, and it was a moment before she had composure enough to speak. "What if Jesus calls?"

I heard the scratchy, distant voice in my mind, and I realized I now remembered it more distinctly than I did Harry's.

"Don't answer." I rolled over and remained wide awake until 7:30 the next morning. Then the phones began to ring and ring, Santa laughed and laughed, all of it on and on, and we clutched each other, straining to hear what our son once heard, wondering who he was calling now.

This Last Thing

For months after Martin died, I was short of breath. None of the grief books friends pressed into my hands—always surreptitiously, like they were palming a bribe—had anything to say about it.

To Brandy, a friend of Martin's whom I'd inherited along with everything else, the answer was simple and came as she pushed past me into the apartment: "Open some damn windows, Peter!" It had been almost a year at that point, and she'd stopped over to help me clean out his clothes. It wasn't his clothes I needed help with, though. There was this other thing.

As for the windows, I hadn't opened any for the same reason I'd put off cleaning out Martin's stuff. His sickness, death, and this—whatever it was, afterlife—had all been a story of attrition. I kept losing more and more of him: then he died: then his body disappeared out the door: now his clothes would disappear with Brandy. And opening the windows here in the apartment, that would mean erasing those places in various closets and drawers and cabinets where I could still smell him. The smell of his sweaters, shirts, jeans, things I'd folded away clean. The smell of his cologne. His favorite toothbrush—though we'd long ago abandoned it in favor of the disposable, Q-tip–style "toothettes" hospice provided—even that had a smell. And in certain corners of the house, down low, behind the couch or the bedroom door, on the floor behind the beloved TV, I imagined I could smell the underlying scent of Martin himself—just a hint, but distinct.

Martin always said Brandy had the personality of a track pistol. She was loud, harmless, and she got things started. (Automatically clever, he wrote for television, but for shows that, like almost everything else of his, are gone now.) Lord knows he could bear her better than I. Still, after the fog of recent months, I was relieved to sit and watch her work with unexpected tact through Martin's belongings, sorting out what to keep and what to donate. There was nothing, really, to keep. Pictures, jewelry. She dove into my closet, my clothes, and culled. "I thought gay men knew how to dress," she called out, her voice muffled by clothes, Martin's and mine, that were all too big.

That's something to toast, Martin said near the end, though it wasn't, and he couldn't, so we didn't.

"What the heck is *this*?" she asked, emerging with Martin's official Wisconsin cheesehead hat.

Living with a writer, especially a television writer, causes you to see the world for the script that it is, to know that what seem like surprises are always predetermined, that for every prop there is a punch line.

"When you say Wisconsin, you've said it all." That was the line. Martin's line. The state's. He never wore the hat, but always sang these words; he went to school at Madison, and apparently this was some sort of fight song. He loved football. He loved cheesy. Needless to say, he stood out in Los Angeles. So did I. I was pale, liked suits, majored in business in college, and was in business until I met Martin.

Brandy did not stand out in Los Angeles. There were hundreds, thousands, like her. With thrift store couture, beautiful teeth, so much hair, notes to herself or to Martin or to me on the backs of outdated headshots (she was no longer an aspiring actor, but an aspiring set designer), she was probably thirty. Or thirteen. I was over forty, or so I told people. And Martin, fifty-two last March and forever the youngest of all of us, never seemed to care.

Neither did Brandy, not when it came to cleaning closets. A new Hefty bag billowed between her hands; in went the hat. A sharp corner of the cheese wedge strained through the plastic accusingly as she disappeared back into the closet.

Eventually, I thought, she'd find it (again, the script), and sure enough, Brandy reemerged on cue, holding a brown shoebox in one hand, its lid in her other, a frown on her face.

And in the box, the balloon. I knew it, though I couldn't see it. Brandy sat down next to me on the bed, held the box in her lap, and waited for me to say something. She herself did not say a word. She was a kind of idiot savant of tact: grace and propriety could steal over her in a rush and leave just as quickly. But during her moments of calm, she was brilliant, and you wanted to collapse into her.

The balloon, twisted and clothespinned at the throat, was a dull red and weakly held about an eggful of air.

This prop, too, had a story, but it wasn't funny. In part because it wasn't a prop. It was a real and terrible thing, a last thing. And there was the problem, or part of it, of me reaching for a word and coming up only with *thing*. Martin would have done better. Actually, he had.

"This," I began and stopped. "There was this writer," I tried. "Do you know her?" I realized I hadn't uttered her name. "Eudora Welty," I went on. Brandy shook her head. "Me neither. But he knew her—*of* her—loved her, and so there was this story of hers."

"I know it!" Brandy shouted. "*The Red Balloon.* The boy in Paris. That movie! It's so sweet, really, that he—"

And that would have been so sweet, really, had that been the story, but it wasn't. Not at all. There was no other way to do this, apparently, than directly.

"No," I said and took the box away from her.

"Peter."

"So this—" I reached into the box, fully intending, but failing, to pick the balloon up. I just looked at it and she did too. "It's his last breath."

"I don't understand," Brandy said.

"Neither did I. But—remember that funny reading group he was in? The one at the library with all the old ladies? Well, just before he got sick, really sick, and couldn't go, they'd finished this collection of short stories. Eudora Welty's. I think it was their third time through.

He was always pushing Welty. He loved her. She went to Madison, too, apparently. Ages ago. Doubt she ever owned the cheese hat. But he'd— this group at the library, they'd push Patricia Cornwell, he'd fire back with Welty. Anyway, in one of these stories, one of the characters dies, and his wife saves his last breath in a little toy balloon." Brandy was smiling now, with teeth bared; grace had fled. "Don't you remember how he was?" I asked. "He loved this idea."

It was so out there, so weird, but at the support group, other caregivers were talking about buying pints of raspberries their loved ones wanted but could never eat, cigarettes they couldn't smoke, CDs they couldn't hear. So when he, when Martin, toward the end, made me go out, buy balloons? I went. I humored him. Again, the wrong word.

"I mean, I first bought balloons with words—funny shapes—he wouldn't have any of that. This was serious. Plain, red, round. Had to be. And we had to practice. This balloon versus that balloon."

I saw that, not unlike that foam cheesehead, something that might seem silly or tender within the intimacy of a couple could become pathetic, even monstrous, when it was exposed to light and air. Who could understand us? Some days, even before he got sick, I couldn't. I didn't work; I didn't have to. I understood it made financial sense. And that it made sense for me to cook and clean. A *stay-at-home spouse*, Martin called me, always with a smile. A *kept man*, whispered others, also smiling. Either way, the joke was always on me, never more so than in those final days, when I kept Martin, when the world had shrunk so small, until it was just four walls, a window, a bed, a man dying, another beside him. It wasn't even terrible, not until the very end.

"He wanted to do this," I told Brandy. "Of course I did what he asked."

I have had time to think about this, time to decide that what he was asking was not to die alone. And asking me to capture his last breath meant asking me to stay by his side, to the last, to count down the minutes and the hours, ever vigilant that this breath—or this one—or tonight's or tomorrow's—might be the last. For a few days, I panicked over the practical aspects: How could I be sure which breath was the last breath? How would I know when Martin was really, and finally, dying? But I was just looking to be distracted by logistics. At the end, hardened with the wisdom the dying grant constant companions, I knew. I told no one else, but I knew. Martin would make it through the night, see the morning, and then—after lunch, definitely before dinner—I knew it was time for him to die. And he did.

I looked at Brandy. All this talk of breath had her holding hers. "That's what he wanted; that's what I did," I said. "I caught his last breath in the balloon."

I exhaled. Brandy did not, though. She was out of her depth and looking it, hair frizzed and floating above her, and when she spoke, she could only get out two words before stopping: "This is—"

I waited. Then I spoke. "A problem, I know." And the problem was this. It wasn't the balloon in the box between us, but the smile, or dim outline of one, attempting to settle on my face. Martin often claimed—and I knew Brandy agreed—I hid behind humor. I was glib when glib wasn't called for. And they were right. But what I'd been doing, holding my breath for weeks, now months, that couldn't be right either.

Nor could throwing away this balloon, its box. Martin had promised his body to the medical school, insisted that they not return his remains when they finally were done with him. This was all that was left of him. *This* he wanted saved.

"Did he say what he wanted you to do with the balloon, after, you know—?" Brandy asked.

"He did not," I answered. "He wasn't all that lucid when he started on this bent."

"But Peter, this is just so *weird.* Martin's last breath, he's, he's *in* there. It's not like some dead—ashes. That's *him* in there. *His* molecules. You *have* something here, something to, I don't know, *honor.*"

I rolled my eyes, but the truth was, I had thought about it: burial, even cremation—the box, the balloon, there'd be something, some debris, after. But that would be even sillier than a balloon in a box. Sillier than a man left as its caretaker. Sillier than the man who'd inspired it. Martin: *The word "inspire" originally meant "to breathe."* Who would tell me that now? All I had now was Brandy, and *molecules,* which made me want to laugh (again, citing Martin: *"K" sounds are always funnier; "pickle" always beats "pear"*) and because of that, cry.

Fortunately, Brandy's subsequent ideas, all ridiculous—Griffith Park at dawn, kayaks off Malibu, a trained hawk—prevented any real tears. It had been like this for months, tears en route, only to lose their way. And then Brandy suggested we visit her shaman.

"Brandy," I said.

"His name is Wiggy," she said.

So no tears, but no laughs, either. Once upon a time I would have laughed, but my emotions of late ranged from despair to anger, the gradations of which my mind seemed to select via slot machine—always random, the only jackpot, as now, a bright, clanging fury. "Please, Brandy, please. This is one of the reasons he and I hauled all the way east to old-money Pasadena. No LA foolishness like—like shamans." Brandy turned away, hurt. "Brandy." I extended a hand. Now I was consoling her: like I said, she's a kind of genius.

Truly: "He's from *Wisconsin*," she said and led me out the door.

The shaman, of course, lived—worked? shamed? shammed?—in Santa Monica, right off the Third Street Promenade. Everyone who's not from here lives there. Not necessarily in Santa Monica, but near the beach. It's what the rest of the country thinks Los Angeles is. A beach town. It's not. It's Pasadena, which is to say, a bunch of old orange groves abutting mountains, no water in sight.

"We don't have to call first?" I asked as we parked. "The shaman's always open?"

Brandy giggled. "Peter, you are so—Pasadena. It's cute." I told her I felt kind of ill, and I did. Martin's box weighed more, was warmer than when we started out. It was like we'd traveled to one of the heavier planets.

Wiggy looked upset when he opened the door. A Cher-like woman lounged in a large papa-san chair that was visible in the room behind.

"Shaman Wiggy," Brandy pleaded, shooting glances at Cher. Probably thought it was Cher. I took another look. Maybe. "This is major big. We're talking life and death and the Journey of Souls," she continued, and you could hear the capitalization, or at least, Wiggy could: he opened up.

There was no place to sit. The walls were painted brown, shopping bag brown, and the ceiling, white. It made you look straight up.

"When you turn out the lights, it's a sky full of stars," Brandy whispered to me, twinkling a bit herself.

Wiggy sat like a trained bear on a footstool next to Cher. He looked like Jerry Garcia. And Ben or Jerry. And my aging hippie mailman who still delivers mail for Martin, even though I've asked him not to: gray beard, smoked glasses, serape, huarache sandals, these short pants—knickers? culottes? What was the word? I looked down to Martin's balloon for confirmation; Wiggy caught me.

"What's in the box, bro?" He coughed lightly. Cher frowned like she didn't do shoeboxes. She was very tall. She had it going on, really: the height, the hair, the eyes. She rose and walked toward the kitchen. Small apartment. Martin would have *loved* this. Loved it. He wrote scripts for what he called "Ambien TV"—that 12 to 5 a.m. stretch that belonged to insomniacs, to infomercials, and to Peter Falk and other stars who, every time you saw them, made you think: *Are they dead?* Martin would have had this Brandy adventure on the air pronto. Saturday-night movie showcase. *Beach Shaman Shootout.*

"Friend," Wiggy asked again and pointed. "In the box?"

Brandy looked at me, saw I wasn't going to respond—*What? He's a shaman*, my eyes told her, *let him figure it out*—and spoke up herself. "Peter's lover died," she said, eyebrows raised. Wiggy nodded expertly. "And now he has a problem," she said, and now I did.

Brandy explained what was in the box, and Wiggy's eyes went a little wider. So did mine.

"How'd it work?" Cher called from the kitchen. She had the smoky, dark, impatient voice, too.

"Yeah, like, how'd you do that?" Wiggy asked. "Very cool, if you don't mind my saying."

Brandy looked at me.

"Uh," I said and stopped. That seemed like enough. And there's no way I could have told them, told them everything.

"He just caught it," Brandy said.

Martin might have been able to improve on Brandy's line, but not Wiggy's reaction. He was open-faced, professionally interested, and not—like those orange-apron guys in the aisles at Home Depot. *I have this air pressure problem . . .*

"So," Wiggy said, "we have a spirit that needs release."

Fuck you, I said, or almost said, having pulled that slot lever once again and come up lemons. Brandy looked at me, eyes full. I was touched, even jealous; her tears came so effortlessly. "Listen," I said, starting over. Martin, who didn't write much for cable, argued that swear words, like exclamation points, were a sign of weakness; if you had to use them, it meant you weren't getting your point across! "The thing is," I went on, "why would he have wanted me to save it, only to release it?"

No one said anything.

Wiggy pointed at me and looked around for support. "That is *so* beautiful, man." He shook his head and snagged a set of keys from the floor. "Let's go," he added, face serious, eyes smiling. "Cher-babe!" he shouted into the kitchen. *No way,* I thought. I looked at Brandy. She looked at the box. Cher returned silently, picked up a purse the size of my palm from the papa-san chair, and strode out, wordlessly, ahead of us all. "*Vámonos,*" Wiggy ordered. "Let's go. Beach. *La Playa.*"

I felt foolish carrying the box, which was heavy again, and hotter now, still hotter in the sun. *I'm sorry, Martin,* I thought, because that's when I knew how this would turn out. *I screwed up. I'm really, really, sorry,* I went on, and remembered thinking the exact same thing, the same words, as Martin died. Wiggy dropped back with Brandy.

At the light, I found myself beside Cher. "Sorry," I said, because the word was fresh in my mind, and because, well, the moment seemed right. She just nodded, not looking at me. She was pretty damn close, I will say that. "Sorry," I said again, realizing that something about her was making me say that. "Sorry about Sonny, I mean," I said automatically, which is to say, foolishly.

She stopped. That is to say, we were stopped, standing there, but now everything stopped, and she turned to face me, long and full. I realized, that, if I'd ever known Cher, really known her, why-not-stop-by-Thursday? known her, I'd have known instantly, back in the apartment, if it was really her. But Jesus. She looked at me. She pointed at the box. "Martin," I said, because I didn't know her, and she didn't know me, or Martin, or because I hadn't said his name aloud for how long now? So long. Since the very last time. My legs turned to wind. They were no longer there, not holding me up; my body was twisting and alive again. "Martin," I repeated, just to myself, but it wasn't the same, but I had the memory of saying it aloud all the same, the syllables, letters, spilling out across my lips into human air, where humans heard them, and a man named Martin, a man I loved, might have answered and smiled, and breathed, and come across the room with a kiss.

"I'm sorry," Cher said.

"I'm sorry," I said, and the walk signal flashed. Wiggy and Brandy had caught up.

"Let's not miss the light," Wiggy said, and we all crossed together and went down to the sand.

"Peter," Wiggy called, very softly. I listened to the surf. "Are you ready?" I was already crying. Maybe I'd been crying this whole time, the whole walk down, but you think I would have noticed. I hadn't much cried before. Not for months. Everybody said—I know they said, because Brandy told me—"Why didn't he cry? Why didn't he cry at the funeral?" She said some people thought I was being strong, but I think she made that up. People thought I was being a cold bastard.

We were far from the roadway, far from the water. The beach there is so wide: too wide, something beautiful made garish by excess, by too much effort.

He didn't try at all, Martin. I tried. One of us had to. But if only one of us tried, then only one of us lost, and I did, all of him, by degrees—first his T cells, then his flesh and muscle, his will, later his laugh and smile.

Then you throw out his clothes and his stuff and his cheese hat, and then you come down to the beach—and what's left, then? I looked at the box.

"Sorry," I said again, this time to the box, but aloud.

"I know," Brandy said.

"Shut up," Cher said.

"Hey, hey," Wiggy said, very quietly. "Peter," Wiggy said. Brandy was about to say something, but Wiggy stayed her with a hand, eyes locked on mine.

I looked back; I looked at the box. I took a breath. And another. And then a deep, long one, the one you take before beginning, before going under, before the wave crashes over you. A breath deep and low, so I filled with air, so my chest filled and my mind filled with Martin, his chest, meager then—that chest I'd loved, caressed, washed and dressed—that chest swelled to bursting with its last breath, the breath that wouldn't, couldn't come out, because my hand was firmly clamped over his lips.

"Don't fight, Martin," I had said and said now, aloud. "Don't fight." He had days, hours. The doctors had been saying this for months, weeks. Days, hours. How can that be, I'd screamed, at first when he was out of earshot and later, when he wasn't. "We brought him home to *die*," I'd said. "You said we could, and now he isn't, he isn't dying, he's suffering and suffering, and we're all—I'm all—*suffering* with him. *When?*"

The next morning, I knew when. After lunch, in the light he'd loved, at the time he'd loved—one o'clock, *the civilized hour*, he'd always said, the hour he began to write every day. That was the time. I got out the balloon and held it before him like a toy. He looked at me without tears, without a smile, without—so softly, so gently I did this. I drew my hand along his cheek, felt the rough skin, the beard—*I should have shaved him this morning*, I thought, but no, it felt good rough and stubborn. Easier to grip.

I bent to kiss him, and a little puff of air greeted me. His lips did not close to meet mine, but lay there, chapped and still.

O, he said, or something said, in a puff. I looked at him, his eyes. *O*. Still warm, still alive. *Martin*, I said.

O, he said again and puffed.

No, I hushed and clamped. With one hand I held his mouth, pinched shut his nostrils. *Relax,* I said. *I'm not going to let go. I won't let the air escape, I won't.* And, in a single motion, I switched hands and held the balloon in place, its mouth in his, its throat pinched gently between my fingers.

Writers write, Martin had said once when I asked what he was doing, staring out a window. I stared, too. *Viewers view,* he said. And we stared out the window, on and on, it was a cold day, I remember that, and my breath fogged the glass until I leaned back, and it disappeared.

At my lips, the balloon: a whiff of Martin, the touch of wet, chapped lips, the taste of a kiss, the brush of a hand, a scent, like death, but only that, a breath. Then a roar from the wind and the sea, and then nothing, not a whisper, not a sound, not from me.

140 Characters

The old nun, Agnes, who keeps to herself.

The old nun's friend, Frieda, because even old nuns who keep to themselves keep at least one friend, and that's who Frieda is, and why not, because she too is an old nun but also a former one, and was happy to drive over this fine summer evening and help Agnes root around the front yard looking for Joseph, who's not a nun but a saint, or its plastic replica, buried upside down somewhere here in front of the convent, the two old women are sure of it, because the building is for sale and tradition holds that this is what you do: hire realtor, plant sign, bury Joseph, hello buyer. *Is that smoke?*

Suzanne, who doesn't go to church nowadays—Sundays are for open houses—but happily retweets the odd biblical passage she comes across and keeps a trunkful of Saint Josephs rattling around in her car to give to clients: *Hey, you never know . . .*

Her clients, the nuns, specifically Mary Pat and Mary Grace, two of the three women remaining at the old convent in the inner city, who are sitting inside wondering when Agnes, the third, is going to come back from that walk she claimed she was taking, what that high-pitched sound is (it's the smoke detector, there's a fire, a fire), whether their hearing aid batteries need replacing, who will pay for that, and if they really should ask Hector to bury the statue of Saint Joseph in the yard, because they haven't yet.

Hector, who installed the smoke detector that's trying to save the nuns, and who has buried the following things in his own backyard: five mice the poison killed, two the cat killed, and the cat; a chicken neck, a votive candle, and a picture of someone he hated; a chicken heart, a votive candle, and a picture of someone he loved; Mrs. Reynoso's business card with the bright-red palm; two Pic 'n Save Supermarket bags, one inside the other, encasing a Glock he was told didn't work; three hundred U.S. dollars and two thousand Honduran lempiras in an old pickle jar; a startlingly large dead crow he found Tomas and Angelina playing with one morning as he was headed to work at the convent he knew would close soon.

Gladys Reynoso, who attends mass every Sunday in the old convent chapel, sitting in the designated seats for the laity high up in the loft, looking down at the long empty pews below, the designated seats for nuns, wondering where those nuns are, wondering if they buried the secretly extra-special statue she gave that woman Suzanne, who would die very wealthy, Gladys told her, but not that she would die next year, nor that this one particular Saint Joseph, which Gladys gave to Suzanne to give the nuns to give to Hector to bury to sell the convent, had a teeny, tiny curse on it that would render it useless.

Father McGreevy, who says the mass for the nuns and Gladys on Sunday mornings, or thinks he does, he's eighty-eight now if a day and has retired thrice, once as pastor, once as principal of a small and beautiful school in Hawaii, and most recently as chair of the Monday Afternoon Inner-City Interfaith Golf Council, a collection of priests, rabbis, and pastors—three Toms, one Marc, one Mark, a John (on-and-off), an intolerable Sven, and toward the end, that Angelique—who all spent a cleric's most blessedly empty day of the week, Monday, golfing and for whom the group's acronym, MAGIC, was a source of great ironic pride, though Father McGreevy can't remember why or how the acronym worked, because it doesn't, not really, and neither does he, and the golf in Hawaii was so much better, or so he'd read in the Michener book, which was so long he couldn't remember the characters from one page to the next or whether he himself was in the book or not.

Alice, the librarian around the corner, who checked out the Michener book to Father McGreevy, though no longer remembers doing so because it was eighteen years ago and she's never taken an interest in Michener's books coming or going, much less distinguished between the books themselves.

Grace Paley, whose death Alice still mourns, because Alice had a ticket to see her at the auditorium in 1980 but had to cancel in order to take her husband to the hospital for chest pains that turned out to be heartburn, and because Paley writes so lovingly of libraries and librarians in her story "Wants," in which the narrator returns an Edith Wharton book that's also eighteen years overdue, is charged $32, happily pays and says of the librarian, whom Alice has always liked to imagine is herself, "Immediately she trusted me, put my past behind her, wiped the record clean, which is just what most other municipal and/or state bureaucracies will not do," and because Paley's character immediately checks out the book again.

Chester, Alice's husband, who has never read Michener or Paley or Wharton or the man Alice's library is named for, Walt Whitman, and who wonders every Monday, Wednesday, and Thursday night, the nights the library's open late, why Alice hasn't retired yet, because she's eligible, they'd planned for this, she's put in her time, and they were going to go on a cruise because that's the one kind of trip where they don't care how heavy your luggage is and Alice always brings books and Chester would like to go to Hawaii.

Janice, the travel agent who's amazed she still has clients like Chester who still call travel agents.

Donald, her brother, who told her he was taking his share of what they'd inherited from Mom and Dad and investing it in a 1-800-We-Buy-Ugly-Places franchise, for which $100,000 bought you nothing but a call forwarding scheme that sent nearby calls from prospective clients to whatever primary number Donald gave the service, and he gave them the number of a prepaid cell phone he'd bought from a man named Zeni, who ran a gas station, and if the primary number didn't work, which it often didn't, the cause of which was disputed by Donald and Zeni, then the automated marketing service rang the secondary, emergency backup number, which was Janice's work number, which was fine, Donald insisted, because who calls travel agents anymore?

Silvia does, although she thought she was calling a realtor, or not that, but someone who buys homes cheap, fixes them up, and resells them to finer people for a big profit, someone who would do just that for the old convent across the way, which is crumbling, not an expression, not a metaphor, she stressed in her letters to the archbishop, the mayor, her alderman, the other alderman she wishes were hers since he's always in the paper giving a damn, and that pretty woman from the Channel 4 "All 4 You" consumer segments, where they generally get The Man to pay attention, which is what Silvia wants, someone, anyone, to pay attention to the fact that the building is physically crumbling: a brick tumbled from somewhere way up one morning and landed within four feet of the stroller she was pushing Sara around in, which means that the building will go for sale so cheap that some students or pimps or meth labbers will wind up buying it and there goes the neighborhood, unless someone looking to make some honest money buys it, fixes it, and—Silvia loves this next verb and she can't, couldn't, won't, wouldn't say why, because the reason is private and related to sex—*flips* it, whereupon the convent will go to someone who really cares, who will make it into apartments, bring some new families onto the block, which the block needs because Mr. and Mrs. Rodriguez aren't friendly, Mr. Pimentel is too friendly, the old white lady just strange, and the nine kids in the Christian commune or whatever it is are too eager, too excited, to be living in such a poor neighborhood that so clearly needs their help, particularly free toys at Christmas, which Silvia just wants to shove back at them, especially the stuffed white lambs, and say *No thanks* and *We don't need the dusty, dented canned food either* and *If you really want to give the neighborhood a gift, bathe, wear socks.*

Orlando, who tells his grandkids Petey and Truman that the city in Florida was named for him, and who reglazes the commune's windows for free because they're always getting broken.

Emilio, the plumber, who charges the commune 50 percent over his usual rates because he doesn't like the neighborhood and because they never pay anyway.

Esther, the mail carrier, who buys a forty, just the one, each Friday, from José, from Iran, who runs the package store and doesn't drink, not since Frank died.

Ernest, Tom, Kevin, Chip, Rich, Reggie, and two guys who go by nicknames, Legs and Red, who all used to shop at the package store, just for sodas, always sodas, and always wondered about Frank, if he was José's brother or a friend or—and now won't find out because the new lieutenant, whose rank is her name, came on board and declared that firemen shouldn't shop at package stores, not in uniform.

The lieutenant, who tweets as @number53, because she is, and because it's not about her, but the firehouse, which is home to Engine Company 53, and almost no one notices that she extends her sense of discipline to her tweets, which she limits to fifty-three characters: *Change of seasons = change smoke detector batteries.*

The lieutenant's mother, @firemom, who does notice and retweets her daughter's tweets to the world and/or the eighteen accounts she follows or who follow her—@purplerein, @chumash, @granny2go, @47northbargrill, @tl3442, @seniorctrparknrec, @halfoffTuesdays, @mortsmith7, @tellyouride, @cindyloowho, @29palms, @ladygaga, @sarahpalin, @smokey_bear, @readhead9, @firedad, whom she's never met, @number53, whom she has, of course, and @TideMom, for the coupons and that video, which was funny.

Denis, the twenty-two-year-old tech geek the city hired, who doesn't follow anyone because tweeting is for old people and corporations and because he's too busy moving the closed-circuit TV municipal monitoring network online so police and firemen can access it more easily and see stuff like that tendril of smoke climb the screen, which Denis misses because he's under the desk looking for the other end of the yellow cable and finding instead a scratched Jackson Five CD, *ABC*, that someone apparently used as a coaster.

Jackie, Jermaine, Marlon, Tito, and Michael, the Jackson Five, though Denis googles "CD coasters" instead and finds "the Coasters," whose current four-man group (J.W. Lance, Primotivo Candelara, Eddie Whitfield, Dennis Anderson) is much more complicated than the five-man Jacksons, since Wikipedia tells him (Wikipedia tells him everything, has never been wrong) there were sixteen Coasters who came before (Carl Gardner, Billy Guy, Bobby Nunn, Leon Hughes, Adolph Jacobs, Young Jessie, Will "Dub" Jones, Cornell Gunter, Albert "Sonny" Forrest, Earl "Speedo" Carroll, Thomas "Curley" Palmer, Vernon Harrell, Ronnie Bright, Jimmy Norman, Alvin Morse, and Carl Gardner Jr.), and *What exactly is doo-wop anyway?* Denis wonders and asks Google this, too, which means he misses the tendril of smoke becoming a billowing cloud.

John Montemeri, the Merry Weatherman of Channel 4, who once wrote a book for kids about clouds that Alice never displayed because he confused altocumulus and cirrocumulus and nobody caught it but her, which inspired her to do a display of novels with the word *cloud* in the title that she thinks of now as she begins to smell smoke, though it could just be the latest dinner that retired Chester has burned, still stuck in her nostrils, and maybe that should be next month's display, the senses.

Danny, the census worker, who took the job because he needed and needs the money so badly that he thinks twice before calling 911 on his cell because he worries it will count against his minutes and wonders, since he has limited voice but unlimited texts, if he couldn't just text the fire department.

Rachel, the dispatcher who takes the call and knows she'll get marked down on her weekly score sheet because she failed to keep the caller on the line long enough to confirm his location, to explain to the caller that they can't track cellular calls automatically like landline calls, not as fast, anyway, so she hits the blue light to summon her supervisor, Sonia, so they can both rewind, listen, rewind, listen, and take four minutes to parse the recording and thereby find the fire's location, four minutes the fire takes to find the location of the boxes and boxes of candles that Dolores, long dead, a miserly mother superior in the convent years ago, purchased because the feast day of Saint Lucy, their patron saint, is celebrated with candle wreaths, and because the bulk price was so cheap, and because every lit candle meant one less electric light wasting money.

Teresa, the name Dolores gave to the baby who died in her arms before Dolores entered the convent at seventeen. Edgar, the baby's father, who betrayed them both.

Francis, the finish carpenter who built the cabinets in the convent kitchen. Adolph, who dug the first garden and argued that Francis should have put brass, not wooden, knobs on the cabinets because the ladies deserved it. Margaret, the girl the two men fought over eighty years ago. Dahlia, Agnes's grandniece, who bought the fire extinguisher ten years ago and put it in the cabinet Mary Pat and Mary Grace are now fumbling to find.

Liam Callanan

Andy, the passerby who asks Agnes and Frieda, still outside digging for Saint Joseph, if everything is okay.

Gilberto, another passerby, who interrupts to say that it's definitely not, and who interrupts Agnes agreeing that everything is not okay (though she means with the state of nuns today, the plight of historic convents), to ask if there's anything—anyone—worth preserving inside because the building, ladies, is on fire.

Marcus Anthony Taback, Ph.D., author of *A Short History of the Sisters of Saint Lucy in North America, including the Daughter Houses of the West Indies* (New Brunswick, NJ: Lighted Way Press, 1911), the final forty extant copies of which sit in wooden crates in the basement, next to the boiler, a location no one should ever have thought safe, but which is the safest place today as the building burns from top to bottom, meaning that if the firefighters arrive in time and manage not to flood the basement—doubtful—the crates may be later discovered unharmed, allowing the pages to flutter open to the story of Mother Annabelle Macalester, who founded the order with the mission of aiding blind and almost-blind children, and, having found them aid, found they needed schooling as well, *And that,* as she often said, *was that,* which indeed made for a short history.

Dr. Filipello, Taback's dissertation adviser, who advised him to write longer histories about bigger topics, which Taback opposed: wasn't there freedom in restraint, and wasn't it Mother Macalester herself who said of religious life and study that it represented "the freedom and peace of a wilderness existence, a return to the desert that is also a recovery of (inner) paradise"?

No, it was Thomas Merton.

Whom Mary Pat and Mary Grace met once in a situation not unlike the one they are now in, feeling their way down some darkened stairs through smoke, though then it was New York City and in that old hotel run by nuns down in Chelsea, and they were saving money on lightbulbs or there was a blackout or someone hadn't paid the electric, and Mary Pat and Mary Grace were delighted to happen upon Merton, whom they'd heard was in residence, but was suddenly, like them, out on the fire escape, smoking, another surprise, as he'd famously quit.

Lucas, the nine-year-old boy on the sidewalk outside the burning convent who overhears an older woman, red-haired, Russian, say *Too many stairs* and *They are too old and there are too many stairs,* and Lucas thinks to tell her, *This is why I want a fire pole in my house, in any house I ever live in,* but he doesn't and walks on even though he wants to stay and watch and listen, because if he's not home by six, the bad babysitter, the one who comes on Tuesdays, will leave anyway and leave his baby sister Tamika, six, alone in the apartment.

Timothy, the news director, with the tough call to make: the murder investigation on the south side or the in-progress fire on the north side; the murder would fit in with the station's "Our Deadly Streets" campaign but the flames would be better visually, and the scanner says it's still out of control so he sends the Wolf Coach there first.

Ron, who drives the Wolf Coach—the tricked-out van any TV station needs to do live remotes—and hates the north side because the old buildings might as well be built of lead, the way they interfere with the signal, no matter how he carefully he aims the stinger, rising even now from the roof of the truck.

Devin, who rides a fixed-gear black bike he bought for half a month's rent and whose purchase he refuses to regret, whose AmeriCorps project is a hyperlocal community news-and-take-action video blog that he feeds seven days a week with his not-Apple smartphone, and who, when he sees the convent burning, thinks *Justice is served,* not for any particular personal reason but just because, Catholics, you know.

And Desmond, who does know, who is haunted still by what happened to him so many decades ago—and who knows?, maybe the resulting splintered childhood is why he's living in this crappy neighborhood today instead of Hawaii, retired, with wealth beyond measure—and yet still feels a call to run up the stairs, ahead of the firemen, who are only now arriving, and yank open the door and head for the central staircase, calling, *Let me hear you, let me hear you yell.*

And Trixie, which is not her name, just what Ron, Merry John, Timothy, Chas the weekend anchor, and most of the station call her behind her back, who hears Desmond calling and turns to Ron and says, *Oh God, there's people in there, I can hear them screaming,* which Ron interprets as *Hurry up, we're missing good audio,* and so he only says in reply, *Give me a sec,* though he knows he'll have longer than that, five minutes, maybe, while she does her hair, finds someone to talk to, and then, just before air, per the new guidelines, tweets the breaking news.

Liam Callanan

Agnes and Frieda prize open the front doors in time for Mary Pat and Mary Grace to tumble out, followed by Desmond, who has rescued them and, in so doing, rescued some lost piece of himself, and they all lose themselves in the crowd as the building burns, brighter and brighter and brighter.

Patricia, who knows they call her Trixie but keeps this—and that she speaks three languages, was a Rhodes scholar, ate two bagels this morning, is six years celibate—all to herself, because not everyone needs to know every detail of every other individual's life, no matter how set the current world seems on disproving this.

Patricia, who finds no one to talk to, because she's busy staring at her station-issued, last-legs Blackberry, preparing her tweet, thumb-typing, untyping, retyping, trying to stay within the limits, trying to stay focused, and failing, because for her the story is always elsewhere, like that woman walking down the other side of the street this very moment, ignoring them all and the cloudless sky from beneath her bright-red umbrella: *And that's 139,* she thinks.

Patricia, who looks up and sees the For Sale sign, and thinks, *That's the story,* who sees the boarded-up school just beginning to burn next door and thinks, *That's the story,* who sees herself bent to her phone, hands folded in front of her as if in prayer, and knows *that's* the story, and its protagonist is her one constant and most annoying friend, Anders, her name (and why don't others have a name?) for the pinched, angular cursor that endlessly, mercilessly blinks out at her from whatever screen on which she types, as now, as she wonders, worries, marvels at what we miss, of this world, of others, of the ones below or above, when we reduce our stories to 140 characters.

Paper War

WE WERE BOTH OF US FOOLS.

It was not infectious; we came by our predicaments independently. Me: Yale sophomore, on a scholarship, majoring in classics until I dropped out in late 1944 because a treasured mentor said, "Get thee hence." "Hence" was the Office of Strategic Services, or OSS, America's newly invented spy service, which was hungry for linguists, even in Greek. But after some hurry-up training on the grounds of the Congressional Country Club in Bethesda, Maryland, my assignment was switched from the land of Achilles (which I *knew from*, as my young students would now say) to the lair of a wayward OSS officer in Alaska. "Put a goat in a stallion's stall and you'll calm it," I was told, "and he needs calming." The "he" was Thomas Geohagan, a captain to my lieutenant, a high school dropout to my college dropout. But he had been a beat cop and I had never beaten anything; in any case, OSS ranks in those days were like doughnuts: the fancier ones went to the people who grabbed them first. And Alaska in those days was like it is these days, a frontier that devours the cautious and incautious alike.

But Geohagan. He was short, five nine, and had the build and complexion of a tree blown bare by the wind. Red hair, red face, red rage. He had huge hands, which looked menacing even at rest, and he was never at rest. Once a beat cop, always a beat cop, I suppose, although there was no chance he would walk a beat after the war. For reasons I had to sleuth out on my own, Geohagan, in addition to his fancy rank, had earned himself a wooden leg for some previous service rendered. Another discovery: though I initially took him to be my rough equal in age, I later learned he was almost two decades older.

But that is not a secret. Neither is how he died, nor where. But why he died, hardly twelve weeks before the war itself came to an end, and by whose hand, that is a secret.

Or so I thought.

Ghosts come to us in many forms, and when one has reached an age as advanced as mine, ghosts come to make up the majority of one's acquaintances. Not a surprise.

But it was a surprise to find myself haunted by a recent letter from a former student, and not because of the infelicity of his prose.

Dear Professor—and here he misspells my name—*I don't know if you remember me*—and I do not, I am retired—*but I have started a book project, a novel, and it's taken a most interesting turn*—

Among the words Shakespeare might have used to describe his own *Hamlet*—a play, a tragedy, a diversion, an entertainment—I am sure there resides not *project*. And *interesting:* insufficient, but not incorrect, given what my correspondent writes a paragraph or two later, after discussing how he'd found a "treasure trove" of information in the National Archives' OSS files regarding one of World War II's stranger chapters, wherein the empire of Japan developed the planet's first intercontinental ballistic warhead with the help of mulberry paper and potato glue.

And memorably explosive hydrogen.

And all of it combining to create no mere weapon, but a balloon almost five stories tall.

Yes, a balloon. And not a dozen, but thousands. Far fewer than that actually reached North America, but the report of one that did—in distant, all but roadless Bethel, Alaska—caught my student's eye for two reasons.

One, amidst the usual wreckage had been discovered an unusual item: *postcard (1), written in Japanese, in a childish hand.*

Two, the report said I was the one who discovered it.

My student writes, *This seems like a story,* and he is correct. And he asks, *What did it say?*

I shall tell you instead.

I have no idea what Anchorage was like before the war, but I have trouble imagining it even existed. Despite the influx of thousands of men in uniform during World War II, it seemed a vestige of the Wild West, a tiny town where many of the roads halfheartedly trailed off into dirt or gravel after only a few blocks. The population consisted almost entirely of men and dogs, the numbers roughly equal between them, though the dogs were more likely to be sober.

Fort Richardson, just north of town, was slightly less raucous, occasionally less drunk. The base was many soldiers' last stop before the

Aleutians, a vicious theater of war made invisible by both impenetrable weather and equally intimidating press censorship.

Certainly the press never ventured into that far corner of the base where Geohagan lurked. A Quonset hut ringed by a double-height chain-link fence, fringed with barbed wire and monitored by sentries, it looked like any one of dozens of similar buildings. But inside, it was different. A narrow path wound through the vast interior, past heaps of sandbags, towers of crates, cascades of wire and rope, and in a cordoned-off area, tripods with movie cameras keeping careful watch on a row of worktables, each topped with what looked like an iron wedding cake. And dangling from the ceiling throughout, what I took to be tremendous tarpaulins, unlike any I'd ever seen before. The space was ill lit, but even so, I could tell the material hanging was of a delicate, almost spectral construction.

It may seem strange to call attention to the lighting, but something to understand about Geohagan, something I understood far too late, was that his first love was theater. Not that he himself understood this, nor that he would have admitted it if he had. But drama—specifically, *melodrama*—was his addiction, and like every addiction, his weakness. Mine is words. I suppose it was inevitable that we two addicts would one day collide.

So raise now the curtain, see the new actor picking his way through the dark and debris that's always backstage toward the spot Geohagan has carefully illuminated, his "office": a small, confined space demarcated by plywood walls not much more substantial than an actual stage set. This was me, reporting for duty for the first time.

Geohagan was from Milwaukee. Once upon a time. As I've said, a beat cop, albeit one with a special beat, he once explained with some pride: he had been a member of the "Possible Squad." They tackled the hardest cases, cases when you knew who was guilty, but it was impossible to prove. Or there was a gang proving impossible to roust from a particular part of town. Or a fellow officer—a gadfly, say, a real stickler—who was impossibly clean. But it was just two letters—*i, m*—that separated the two words, *possible, impossible*. It wasn't always easy, taking those two letters away—or two teeth, or two fingers, or a body from a dark basement taken out by its own two feet—but it was always possible. That's what

Geohagan told me he told his grateful boss, who was so impressed (or frightened), he said Geohagan should call it the Impossible Squad. Too limiting, was Geohagan's take. And untrue: "Everything's possible."

I suppose the OSS files in the National Archives corroborate this. I have not seen them myself, so forgive me if the potted history I offer now is redundant. Let us start a full year before I reached Alaska, before I was even in uniform. November 4, 1944. A U.S. naval vessel made a curious discovery some sixty-six miles southwest of San Pedro, California. The lookout first reported a downed pilot—what he could see through his binoculars had all the looks of a parachute. But there had been no word of any sorties being flown in their sector that day. Who could this have been? Upon drawing closer, the ship found no evidence of a pilot or plane, and when the material was hauled on board, it appeared to be a large hot air balloon of rubberized silk or some strange paper. Instead of a basket, it contained a peculiar sort of crate, to which were affixed various instruments. One of the communications officers mused that it looked like a weather balloon. Fair enough. The ship's captain brought the balloon and its crate home, where it was packed off to a warehouse in Long Beach. Word was sent to the weather bureau to collect its fallen star.

The bureau had yet to reply when reports of an explosion outside Thermopolis, Wyoming, reached authorities a few weeks later. On December 6, around 6 p.m. Mountain War Time, several residents saw what appeared to be a parachute, though it was rocketing toward earth with fatal speed. Shortly thereafter came the sound of a tremendous explosion; those who'd seen the parachute now saw bright flames of a bizarre red hue leap in answer to the sound. Some set out to discover what had happened, and there, fifteen miles northwest of town, they came upon a great crater littered with shrapnel. The police notified the military immediately.

Five days after, the Fourth Air Force, headquartered near San Francisco and responsible for the air defense of the West Coast, learned a gigantic paper balloon had crashed outside Kalispell, Montana. The construction, though elaborately conceived, was somewhat makeshift, and authorities initially believed it had been assembled and launched from a German prisoner-of-war camp or one of the Japanese internment camps.

But within the next few weeks, dozens of balloons were sighted. Some as far north as Saskatchewan and others just south of Santa Barbara. With great haste, authorities from the various entities involved convened and determined what was happening. Japan had developed and was deploying the first warheads in history that could fly of their own accord from one continent to another. And so far, America's defense consisted of tall trees and wide-open spaces.

During our postwar plunder of Japanese military documents, we would learn that some nine thousand balloons were launched across the Pacific between 1944 and 1945. And though it is thought that fewer than one thousand finally reached America, the threat was still very real. It was not difficult for military planners to imagine the escalating risks. The earliest balloons appeared to contain antipersonnel bombs, and others, incendiary devices. The latter could be deadly enough—the army deployed 2,700 troops across the Northwest as firefighters to protect the nation's most valuable timber stock—but what really frightened authorities were other possibilities, such as biological and chemical warfare: some of these balloons, after all, were dropping right into America's breadbasket. Or the clear psychological threat—what panic would ensue if it emerged that America was unable to protect its citizens, even those farthest removed from conflict, from the enemy's murderous wrath? And finally, so unsettling that it was rarely even mentioned aloud, the balloons might permit—in fact, may have already allowed—Japanese soldiers and spies to sail through our defenses and open a new front behind enemy lines.

Like so many things, what sounds farfetched now was made quite plausible by the dystopia of a world at war. In fact, the Allies *had* experimented briefly with balloons, though few knew of the program. Here Geohagan reenters our story, though not by his own telling. More eager then than I am now to play sleuth, I asked around, I read files I officially should not have, I bought drinks for visiting officers. Please understand: This was my *job*. If not by definition, then surely insinuation. Our OSS training, as brief and inclined to opera buffa as it had been, had made it clear that the enemy we fought was everywhere. Trust no one. Investigate everyone.

And so I came to find that Geohagan had been among the first to investigate these mysterious balloon crash sites—and among the first to discover what the balloons carried. If one particular balloon, the first he found, had not been damaged during the crash, there would have been enough payload to kill him. Instead, he lost his lower leg.

He had been an angry man before the blast, I was told, well

suited to war, and I can attest that losing the leg confirmed his world outlook. And this outlook only worsened when he learned that the U.S. Army Air Forces (USAAF) wanted to discharge him while he recovered.

Geohagan came at them full force, mixing vitriol, some logic (his expertise, a manpower shortage), and a marked aptitude for blackmail. They eventually capitulated, though they dispatched him to distant Alaska, where they imagined someone who could so readily make life difficult for people would identify with a like-minded environment.

Unfortunately for the USAAF, the jet stream—a new discovery—made Alaska a candidate to lead balloon-recovery efforts, and Geohagan's personality made it the center of the universe. Within a few months, he was directing the balloon battle not just in Alaska but also across the United States and Canada, as far as USAAF planes would take him.

Nevertheless, history has ignored him. A Major General Sueyoshi Kusaba is generally given credit for Japan's Fu-Go Weapon operation, as we later learned it was called. But Captain Thomas Geohagan, OSS, is never given credit for the American response, which, given his nature and the methods he employed, is precisely what he desired.

And until this former student of mine came nosing around, I had not received credit—nor blame—for anything related to this campaign, which, I assure you, is as I desired.

My student wants a story. I have told half a one, an eighth of a one, about my thespian captain, Thomas Geohagan. Let my student tell the rest of it. Let him imagine the brawls (with me, with others, with anyone at hand) in the officers' club, let him imagine Geohagan driving a knife through his pant leg into his wooden shin as a kind of party trick, let him imagine Geohagan sticking the wrong shin one night when he'd had too much. Let him imagine my steady mistreatment and, worse yet, my underuse. Let him imagine Geohagan and I dropping out of the sky into town after town, sometimes our plane landing right on some lonely stretch of rural highway, Geohagan bullying witnesses into silence, sometimes with gun, sometimes without, me forever following, explaining, silencing. I was so good at silence. I have always been good at silence. When Geohagan came knocking at night—sometimes we would stay in a motel; sometimes we would pitch a tent—and ask, "Are you there?," I did not answer. But at my peril. I imagine he had made a fierce policeman. Physical. He was persistent. Persistence is not heroism, though, even in wartime, even when it leads to death.

But for the young novelist, this is the story: *I think someone died?*

To put him off the scent, I might say this: *Yes.* And: *Six died.* And: *Reverend Archie Mitchell took his wife and some kids from church on a picnic in the woods near Bly, Oregon. May, 1945.* I will leave you in suspense as to why Reverend Mitchell was not overseas in uniform— because I myself do not know—but I will say at the outset that the reverend did not die. Rather, he dropped the group off on the side of the road to go exploring while he found a better spot to park the car.

But it was the group who found something remarkable. Some apparatus in the trees—or on the ground? The record does not say. Only that four boys (one eleven, two thirteen, the fourth fourteen) were there, and one girl, thirteen, and one woman, twenty-six, the reverend's wife, great with child. If the balloon *had* been dangling there, it would have been mesmerizing, a hypnotist's watch the size of Big Ben, an aircraft that had taken the trouble to fly five thousand miles from a beach in Japan to a forest in Oregon. But what am I saying? A balloon, yes, but a bomb. Was it one of the boys who discovered this first? Boys have a reputation for trouble.

The blast killed the wife and children instantly. That's what most accounts say. But here is my gift to the novelist, what most accounts do not say. The teenaged girl survived long enough for the reverend to come to her side, long enough for help to arrive, long enough to be borne down the mountain. At least partway. I don't know where exactly on the road she died, only that she did. Nor do I know when the reverend later decided to marry one of her sisters, although he did. And finally, while working for peace in the war—one must clarify when speaking of *war* in our bloody epoch; I speak here of Vietnam—the reverend died, in another forest, on another continent. All facts. He disappeared there, not far from the Cambodian border, kidnapped from a leprosarium. What drew him to southeast Asia? What crossed his mind as he crossed the Pacific in the opposite direction that balloon had come hardly twenty years before? Let the novelist say.

I do not recall ever sleeping my entire time in Alaska, though I must have. Actually, I do remember one episode, when Geohagan slugged me awake and threatened worse after I'd begun to drool on him during an overnight flight out of Anchorage to Montana.

Our modus operandi, detailed at slightly greater length: As reports of balloons came into our office, Geohagan would determine with local officials what danger existed of word leaking. As the balloons frequently (fortunately) found sparsely inhabited areas, often all that was required was a rapid-deployment unit from the Fourth Air Force. They would swoop in, recover whatever material remained, and do their best to disguise any lingering evidence. Those places where civilians were involved or, worse yet, the press, would receive a visit from Geohagan and myself.

At first, I thought Geohagan's rough demeanor and clumsy theatrics made him ill suited for such a sensitive job. But it turned out that he was exactly matched to the task and time. This was war, and the domestic public-relations campaign the government mounted had made everyone into a soldier, uniformed and sworn or not. That meant that most times, Geohagan had only to issue civilians a brusque order and know it would be obeyed. It worked time and again, in towns large and small. Again, his days as a beat cop served him well.

And when civilians didn't obey, he always had his well-tended madness to draw upon. I saw him enact his favorite routine again and again, forever unholstering his gun and placing it on, say, the kitchen table or mayor's desk or editor's in-box, telling his quarry they were free to pick up the gun and use it against him, because that would be tantamount to disclosing the secrets they now knew. Over time, I was intrigued to see it worked less well with women, especially old.

But it always worked with men—except once, when a reporter young as I, 4-F and angry as Geohagan, picked up the gun. "What if this was loaded?" the reporter asked. The reporter aimed it at me. "What if I accidentally shot him?"

Geohagan, ham-handed as he was, was at least a professional. Amateurs scared me more, and still do.

"It's not loaded," Geohagan said, "but the lieutenant's having himself a hard war, so if you nicked him clean through the heart, I'm sure he'd thank you." Geohagan waited, and then took the gun away from him, as easily as if he'd been offered it. "I know I would." He checked the cylinder and pretended to be surprised when he was able to eject, one by one, six bullets.

Early on, I confided in some other officers—various military superiors—that Geohagan's tactics made me uncomfortable, but when I told them what I had seen, they sighed with relief. He was capable of far worse, they assured me. The OSS was supposed to be a kind of insane asylum for him—indeed, the OSS had plenty of fellows who would have been, should have been, at home in a real one—as the army had been trying to get rid of him long before he'd lost his leg. He had been an infantryman in the South Pacific and, during one brutal battle, had succeeded in single-handedly clearing out a machine-gun nest manned by six Japanese soldiers. When his CO arrived to inspect the victory, he discovered six bodies, six heads, and six tongues, all arrayed in separate lines. Geohagan explained that he had interrogated the men before killing them. If they did not talk, he cut out their tongues to make that condition permanent. The CO asked him if he spoke Japanese. Geohagan asked why.

I learned never to ask Geohagan why. Why he shot a man's horse in Montana after we had wished him good day and shut the door to his trailer. Why he took a crowbar to a woman's windshield in Arizona, or why he brandished the bar at me when I tried to interfere. He may not have known himself; he seemed to have as much control over his anger as the Japanese their balloons. Sometimes he would mutter that life had been simpler with the Possible Squad. Sometimes he would say this work was even better than the Possible Squad. All that was certain, to me, was the ensuing explosion.

So I did not ask him why he was sending me on ahead of him to a crash site near Bethel, Alaska, in early June of 1945. In truth, the assignment promised to be fairly routine. Lonely Bethel, deep in Alaska's still-unvisited southwest, had had its share of balloons, and we had long since convinced those there who cared that these were merely weather balloons gone awry. And few did care. The town was three-quarters Yupik Eskimo, and few spoke English. This didn't mean they weren't well aware they were lied to all the time: they didn't seem to mind so much so long as you left by nightfall.

The settlement was impossible to reach by road, and possible by boat only in summer. I missed traveling with the advance recovery team, and the Anchorage airfield couldn't spare another aircraft for the sole pleasure of a solitary lieutenant, so I had to fly to Bethel commercially. I was amazed that one could, much less in a plane made entirely of wood. But I could and did and had the passenger cabin, six seats, all to myself. Above me, the pilot had the open cockpit all to himself. He not only kept the engine running when we landed but taxied away as soon as I leapt out, and was airborne before I had reached the fence lining the field. An old man with ink-black hair and a thin mustache was waiting there. Not for me. Just waiting.

I nodded to the disappearing plane: "He was eager."

"Always are," the old man replied, and so our conversation concluded.

They weren't much more talkative inside the small hut that served as the airfield's terminal, but at least I learned that my initial plan—to commandeer a vehicle and drive to the crash site—was ludicrous. No road stretched more than a mile or two past the city limits. No road could: the tundra, frozen solid in winter, was a spongy sea of grass in summer.

But they had heard about the "weather balloon" I was after. A bush pilot from their field had first reported it. He could be found, they said, and he could find the crash site again for me, for a price. I agreed.

The pilot and his amphibious plane were soon produced, but he refused to take me anywhere until I acquired—at great expense from his colleague, who suddenly became the proprietor of a small, exorbitant wilderness outfitter—a survival pack containing a tent and other emergency supplies. I had scared up some C rations before leaving Anchorage, but these were deemed insufficient, and I was ordered to supplement them with several tins of sardines. To show I wasn't entirely the mark they took me for, I went to open one to check for spoilage; the clerk warned, "Be careful with those." But from Geohagan I had learned a healthy disrespect for most cautions and all civilians; key in hand, I peeled back the lid.

They were extremely pungent. I was told this announced not their spoilage but their delicacy.

"Better eat 'em now," the pilot advised. "Because they're not going in the plane."

But they did. Because when I refused to eat them, he eagerly did, and the smell coated the entire inside (and perhaps outside) of the plane thereafter. I can smell it now. And, with equal clarity, I can see the lake he took me to: the water was still, a green-black tablecloth freshly laid. We landed so smoothly I wondered why man had ever bothered with asphalt runways.

The advance detail had frowned up at us as we buzzed the crash site on our approach, and did not find smiles for me as I waded ashore and my plane departed. Something was not right, they explained. The balloon and undercarriage, usually found damaged, were in almost pristine condition. There was no evidence of any explosion, but neither were there any unexploded bombs. This alone was not that unusual—sometimes the bombs fell off and detonated over the ocean—but particularly curious was the compartment where the balloon's crude instrumentation was housed. It was empty. And it was large.

With temperatures in the midfifties, it was balmy for an Alaskan June, but the skies promised worse. The crew was anxious to load everything into their own floatplane—an ungainly PBY Catalina, whose twin overwing props always gave it the look of nervously hunched shoulders—and fly home. They weren't wrong to feel that way. Even someone like myself, someone from Outside (Alaskans' term for the Lower 48, if not the rest of the world), understood the stakes in Alaska, particularly after dark. It wasn't just that the vastness could swallow you up. It was eager to.

But I wasn't eager to return. I had made such an effort to get out there, and the prospect of a prompt return to Bethel, much less Anchorage and Geohagan's dark and crowded Quonset hut, held little appeal.

I told them to leave without me, and explained that I would radio Bethel for a plane to collect me later that night. There was a mystery here; it warranted at least some detective work. And this far north, we had hours of daylight left.

Finally they smiled: *We?*

In the end, they shrugged—OSS officers were always suspect, I had learned, and therefore, expendable—and left me with a radio I soon discovered did not work.

The broken radio meant I couldn't call Bethel for a plane, but no matter. Geohagan had long ago secured for us special radios designed for long distances and classified communications. They were called "cloud radios" in honor of some obscure technological feat. I could never shake the image, however, that I was talking through a cloud whenever I used it, because the quality of Geohagan's scrambled replies was so poor. I had a special "spy camera" as well, to take photographs independently of the recovery team. Its quality, too, was terrible, and I had replaced it with a reliable civilian model.

I dropped my pack, took out my camera, and looked around. Vast stretches of Alaska, particularly in winter, suggested the moon to me, but this spot was different—the moon in the midst of a wet summer. The lake, dark and solid, sat in a large, stony bowl, which was ringed with sharp peaks scabbed with snow. A timid band of green fuzz surrounded the shores of the lake, and here and there, an entering stream occasioned some low brush and, in certain cases, a birch or spruce. The far end of the lake looked inviting; here, where my map told me the lake emptied into the Kuskokwim River, the green gathered itself up into actual trees. Having found nothing much left of the crash site to photograph for Geohagan's greedy eyes, I made for the trees. The hike looked to be short, and I imagined a panoramic tableau awaited. I had been overdue for leave, and now here I was, on vacation.

Once I began paying attention to where I placed my feet, though, I became less interested in the scenery. My Boy Scout days had been brief but acquainted me with a range of wildlife, including bears. Or what we thought of as bears in the Lower 48; the bear tracks I was now studying were much larger than any I had ever seen.

I consoled myself with the thought that, unlike a Boy Scout, I now had a gun on my hip.

Nevertheless, a rustling in the bushes turned me into a tenderfoot scout once again (and not just mentally, but physically: these "bushes," riddled with dark-red berries, all dwarfed me by a yard at least). I backed up, felt for the revolver, and slowly remembered that, unlike a civilian, a grizzly bear would not be intimidated by the sight of a gun, loaded or not. Up to this point, I had somehow traversed all Alaska and much of the West without a bear sighting, though locals had frequently told me what to expect: first you notice the smell, the horrible smell, then you see them, then they see you, and then you shoot them.

So far, all I had was smell. It was foul, but not—inhuman.

A flash of black hair appeared amidst the bramble, but disappeared so quickly I discounted it. Then a broken twig, but just one, which struck me as odd—surely the bears were not so stealthy. Then I saw him.

He was just a boy, and though I have tried to forget what he looked like, especially his face, my memory is obstinate and recalls every detail with merciless, photographic accuracy. His hair was black, alternately matted and spiky, and his face was discolored with bruises and dirt. His eyes were dotted each with a perfect drop of black. His cheeks suggested they had once been round, but hunger (as I was soon to learn) had pulled the skin taut. He had on a khaki snowsuit, the left leg of which ended in tatters. Before I could take this in, however, he was running directly at me, screaming, fists high. My hand snapped again to my gun. I thought to run, but embarrassment steeled me, and I stood my ground.

As it was, he collapsed a few yards short of me. For a full minute, I did not move. I watched his back rise and fall in soundless sobs. I crept closer. He was not Caucasian, but I had seen enough of Alaska to know, or guess, that he was not Eskimo. An impossible truth slowly took shape in my mind: He was the enemy, Japanese. But—just a boy?

As each moment passed, the drama—and horror—of his situation became clear. The balloons could reach heights where the cold could kill a man, if the lack of oxygen did not. This boy had survived.

I withdrew, came to my senses and opened my camera bag, where I had stashed some of the C rations. I tore them open, removed the cigarettes, and set the food gently between us, as though I were coaxing a stray. He studied me, but only for a moment, and tore into the meal.

I cleared my throat to say something—or rather, to give me time to think of something to say—and that was enough. He scooped up everything left and ran back into the bushes.

I followed him, but to no avail. The bushes soon gave way to a thick grove of pine trees. Everything was now dim and quiet, as eerie as a decommissioned church. How could I be so sure he was alone?

I could not, I decided, and retreated to the lake, back down the shore to where I had left my gear. It wasn't night and wouldn't ever truly be, but the encircling ridge had left the lake in shadow. My equipment was covered with a thin sheet of moisture.

It was possible that I was hallucinating. Entirely possible. I had not had much to eat or drink. And Geohagan occupied so much of my mind in those days that there was little room left in my head for myself. There was certainly none for a Japanese boy, however small.

And yet, not long after, here he came, picking his way up the beach until he was within ten yards of me. Then he stopped. I stood, which he seemed to take as a cue. He canted his head apologetically, spoke, and gave a short bow. I'm quite sure that's when Geohagan would have taken the opportunity to kick his jaw apart, but I did the only thing it seemed I could do in that moment. I bowed as well. (Or rather, I did not bow as *well* as he did. But bow I did.)

This must have called for a toast, for he raised a tiny silver canteen dripping with water and took a sip. When I didn't do anything, he extended the canteen to me.

I wasn't sure what would now be more rude—that I refuse his canteen or that I not come up with my own container to reciprocate? I found a cup in my pack and dipped it into the lake. He smiled at this, and shouted. He dipped his own canteen into the lake. We raised our drinks to each other and drank. He laughed, a tiny scratchy laugh that ended in series of tinier coughs.

Obviously, I was miserable. Not only was he real, but he was alive. Not only was Japan sending balloons across the Pacific laden with bombs; they were ballasting them with children.

Not only had I toasted the enemy; the enemy was a boy.

But how? Was this by design, or accident? We'd learned that children were involved in the production of the balloons: children were light enough to walk across the balloon's paper shell, or envelope, without damaging it; their fingers were small enough to interconnect the intricate fixtures inside; they were the only labor left on the home front. But would the Japanese army really—would they do this?

More to the point: what was he supposed to do now?

As he devoured another C ration, I ran through dozens of other questions before confronting the one that loomed largest: What would Geohagan do? A human—a little boy—was not so easily carted off and hushed up as a partially destroyed balloon was. A story could be invented, but plausibility would stretch past the breaking point. And before all that, basic logistics: How would I get him back to Anchorage? I could hardly smuggle him aboard a floatplane in a sack, and even if I did, to what end? Unzip the bag at the end of a runway back at the base and bundle him off to our Quonset hut? Or, take him to some lonely corner of the base, point in the direction of blackout-darkened Anchorage—or to Canada—or the North Pole—or the Pacific he'd just crossed—and tell him to run?

The boy began a short speech. An explanation, if I had had to guess. His hands went back and forth, up and down, and he finally pointed back to the bushes where we'd first encountered each other. A question was asked.

If it was *Isn't that where we met?* the answer was yes. If it was *Would you like to go back into the trees?* the answer was no.

I told him that I didn't understand, and he nodded, pointed back toward the bushes and spoke loudly.

Yes, I nodded, because it is always easier to tell children this, and he smiled now, bowed quickly, and ran away.

I turned my attention to the lake, where I watched the solutions surface one by one. Simplest would be for me to walk away. The floatplane would come, I would wade out and climb aboard, and fly off. The boy would be left to vanish into memory—or return to the folds of my imagination, if, in fact, that is from where he first sprung. I tried not to think of what lay behind this plan—starvation, hypothermia, grizzlies—but the alternatives eventually all led to Geohagan, which would only be worse.

No, this was the smartest solution for all concerned—cowardly as it was. The boy had faced certain death in the balloon. My interference would—I suppose the word is *upset*—the natural order of things. The longer he was out of sight, the less certain I was that I had ever seen him at all.

I call again in my defense the Last Frontier and all its magic. Have you ever seen the aurora borealis? Let scientists explain the phenomenon all they like. If you have seen the northern lights, you know they are completely inexplicable, unjustifiable, wondrous. A land that permits the sky itself to tear loose and flame is a land that allows anything.

Including, in that sad instant, a whistle. The boy was returning, and this is how he was announcing himself. His age dropped with every bleat. I had taken him for ten or nine, but as he emerged from the trees, I thought eight. As he stumbled and fell, seven. As he finally reached me, panting, and with great ceremony drew a postcard from his pocket, I had no idea whatsoever. Six? Does it matter? I took the card. There was an ink-wash picture of a mountain on one side. On the other, Japanese characters, a handful, handwritten. I knew the kanji for "bomb" but was otherwise illiterate. I didn't understand a stroke of what he'd given me, but I nodded. He smiled. And from one eye, a single tear, and another from the other. He kept smiling. I kept staring, and finally, having tucked the card away, held out a hand. But instead of shaking it, he took it up, as though we might walk somewhere together.

So we did. We walked past my pack along the lakeshore, and I explained things. Alaska, and war, and aviation. What we knew of Japan's balloon program and what we didn't. Wind patterns. Timed fuses. The notion of suing for peace. Of fighting to the last man. Of what a beat cop did, or might do.

He nodded and listened, or maybe he didn't, but he didn't let go, not even when I began to tell him about Geohagan. The boy couldn't possibly understand, I told him, not because he didn't understand my English but because no one could possibly understand Geohagan. My drama-driven theory was a start, but also let Geohagan off too easily. When Gloucester gouges out the vile jelly of his eyes onstage, it's not real blood; the man playing the part doesn't really go blind. But Geohagan: those soldiers, those tongues. That blood was real. And the blood he drew from me, from others—yes, much more minor, but no less viscous, no less bright.

And watching a play, even one whose end you have yet to learn, you can still be certain that it *will* end.

Not so with Geohagan. On- or offstage, I couldn't predict what mood would storm over him when. Plenty of people would have told me that I was enjoying a soft war—a roof, a bed, sheets, running water, hot meals, nobody but Geohagan shooting anything anywhere around me. But such people didn't *understand*—they didn't understand Geohagan; they didn't understand me. The OSS wanted me for better. My professor had promised better. Yale prepared me for better. I *deserved* better.

My God, what a fool I was. That, and worse.

We returned to my pile of gear. The boy set himself to skipping rocks on the lake while I tried to raise Geohagan on the cloud radio. This pricked the boy's interest and he came over to watch. I tossed a stone into the lake to distract him, but he would have nothing of it. Perhaps he was indeed a committed spy. I scanned the skies for a plane. A new plan would have to present itself, and very quickly.

After five minutes, I called again. Nothing.

I kept at it for an hour, the only benefit of which seemed to be that the boy lost interest and went back to skipping rocks. Eventually

I heard what initially sounded like the floatplane returning. When it failed to come into view, I turned again to the radio and realized the faint roar was emanating from there. I adjusted the controls and put out my call again. This time, I heard Geohagan reply through the roar. We exchanged coded greetings, and then he started in.

"Why . . . didn't . . . you . . . come . . . back?"

I could barely hear him, though I was certain he was shouting.

"Significant find," I shouted back. The boy looked at me, wide-eyed. I tried not to look at him.

Geohagan replied: "Advance . . . detail . . . reported . . . situation . . . normal . . . nothing . . . there . . . what . . . discovery?"

I thought about this for a moment. Even though these cloud radios were Geohagan's special delight, I was unsure if he would trust them with the kind of sensitive news I was about to transmit. "Unique, ah, phenomenon," I said.

"Talk . . . straight . . . Ivy . . . League . . . numbskull," came Geohagan's reply.

"Discovered—passenger. Human. Child."

I could not make out his reply, though it sounded like a question—a terribly excited question. I guessed at the answer he wanted and shouted, "Alive!"

Geohagan drilled me on all the particulars. He sounded disappointed and then intrigued when I gave my best guess as to the boy's age. He nevertheless insisted on calling the boy the "pilot," to the degree that I wondered if he had actually heard me say what I'd said: "Estimate six years old." I thought this once again when he asked if I had "worked him over." I asked him to repeat.

"Interrogate . . . him," he roared. "Have you interrogated him? If . . . necessary . . . use . . ."

I waited. But there was only one word to say and it was my place to say it. I shouted, "No!" and I was conscious of how my tongue moved as I said it: what words could one say that made the tongue easy to snatch, hold tight, and slice off?

"Don't . . . fucking . . . move," he said. "Secure . . . enemy. Wait . . . for . . . me . . . for plane . . . first light."

Enemy. What was true was that this couldn't be true. I was privy to the intelligence reports, the analysis. The balloons went too high, were too small. They *killed* children; they didn't carry them. I hadn't seen the boy arrive in the balloon. I had no idea how he'd arrived, but that wasn't my problem, only that he was here.

So I told Geohagan what I thought, and when I said the word, just the one, I instantly knew I was referring not just to the boy's journey but to the boy himself: "Impossible!"

Indeed, it was entirely likely that I had lost my mind.

The cloud radio chose to broadcast Geohagan's reply with perfect clarity: "Everything's possible!"

I decided the end of the lake made for a better campsite than the bare spot where I'd first waded ashore, so I shouldered my pack and started walking. The boy followed immediately. He had been wary of me after I finished talking with Geohagan, but as time passed and no one else appeared, he grew comfortable, as if confident we were now in cahoots together.

I was now glad that Bethel had forced upon me those survival stores. I did not have much food remaining, but I did have a tent, a first aid kit, and a decent knife. The dewfall made building a fire difficult, but in time I had one burning. During my preparations, the boy flitted about the brush and trees in a kind of hide-and-seek, or maybe cowboys and Indians. I wondered if he was playing a contemporary version, whether his bad guys were moon-faced fellows like me.

I meted out another C ration, as what would pass for night—a stalled, gray-tint gloaming—arrived. Though my own stomach burned, I allocated only cigarettes to myself. I half thought not to feed him again—I imagined that so much food, so foreign, would eventually upset his weakened body, and terribly. But when he again looked my way, I didn't hesitate. The sardines. I cracked a tin open, and the smell subsumed us. The boy winced, but ate a bit of it, and then a lot, pausing occasionally to deliver short monologues, each as incomprehensible as it was earnest. His speech seemed to thin after a while, and after a few parting words, he was curled up, fast asleep by the fire. I tossed the sardine can into the woods. I thought of carrying him into the tent, but didn't want to wake him, incite further speech. I needed time to think.

I worked my way through another half a pack of cigarettes—far beyond my usual allotment, which queasiness confirmed. Eventually,

I stoked the fire a final time and, discovering I felt uncomfortable sleeping in the tent, made my own bed by the fire.

The bear awoke us about an hour later. I heard the animal first—it had found the sardine can I tossed away. The boy ran to my side, and then behind me. The bear gave us a glance, but went back to the sardines. He quickly finished and looked up, offended at the meager portion. He seemed to focus on the boy, and of course: the boy reeked of the fish, too. The bear started walking toward us, then broke into a lumbering gallop. I searched my pack for my gun.

Suddenly, the boy's sharp whistle blasted, startling the bear and me both. For a moment, the boy's gambit seemed successful. The animal slowly moved off. Emboldened, the boy blew the whistle again, and now the bear turned. The animal lowered its head and shoulders, and let out a low, guttural growl.

Somehow, my gun was now in my hand. This would be the first time I would fire the weapon away from the base's range (where Geohagan had insisted I take remedial lessons). I was trying to figure out where or what to aim at when the boy blew the whistle again and the bear charged.

I fired.

The boy ran screaming. The bear kept coming. It took two additional shots to stop the beast, and another one before I was certain he was dead. After a few minutes the boy returned, his sooty face streaked with tears. He looked at me, and then the bear, and then he did a strange thing. He walked over to the corpse, as if to touch it. I grabbed him with my free hand.

He wrestled away from me, spat words rapid and dark, and turned back to the bear. I aimed at the carcass, just in case. The boy nudged the bear's back with a single finger. Nothing. He looked at me and wrinkled his nose. The bear stank, and the smell was extraordinary, rather worse than the warnings.

The boy came around to the bear's head. I'd caught the bear over his left ear with one of my shots, and that side of his face was a bloody marsh, already drawing flies. The boy reached out his hand again, to—I want to say that he *petted* the bear, and maybe he did, but that seems insufficient a word. He turned his hand over and let his knuckles graze the bear's fur. I watched him, for a long time—so long it wasn't until I realized that the rising cold around us meant the fire had gone out. I let the boy be and went to stir the coals. Once I had flames again, I waved him back over to the fire, but he wouldn't come. Finally, he withdrew his hand and stood back a step. He refused to look at me as he walked back, and pulled his blankets off to a new location, distant from the bear, and from me. I saw him lie down and later heard him fall fast asleep.

A short time later, another bear appeared, and I realized I had mistaken the fallen bear for one of great size. This new bear was tremendous, but I had a better sense of it, as it managed to rear up and—I would use the word *growl* again, but truthfully, it shouted. The boy popped awake, and I moved my eyes back and forth from the boy to the bear. The bear caterwauled again, but I held my fire—I had only two shots left.

The bear dropped to all fours, nosed the dead beast, looked at the lake, and lumbered away. We both watched its departure, and the boy subsequently moved his blanket closer to me. He must have been very young indeed, for he somehow found himself able to fall fast asleep once again.

I must endeavor now to put into words that for which there are no words, or have not been, for almost sixty years. I must describe what it was like there, in the dark, wracked with nausea from nicotine and shame. Let me take a novelist's palette—and daub from it some freezing temperatures, a bluing sky, the corporal corruption of cigarettes and lack of food or sleep—but only to show you how insufficient a writer's tool it is, only able to paint the external scene. The trial itself took place in my head.

These were the facts. I had shot a bear. I tried to claim self-defense, but the massive mound of him lying there seemed a horrible waste of a life more powerful and productive than mine. To deepen my shame, I recalled the number of bullets it had taken me to fell him. Obviously, I was a horrible shot; his agony must have been extreme. Is this melodrama? Yes. Have you ever killed such an animal? With respect to most, I dare say no.

What else? I had told Geohagan about the boy. And here the drama sharpens. I had had the opportunity to evade Geohagan, to deceive him, and yet I did not. As a result, Geohagan would descend shortly, usurping what little control I still had of the situation.

But the gravest crime was one that I had not committed, not yet, though its taking place seemed quite inevitable.

I had killed a little boy.

How can a man as old as I still indulge such histrionism? This is how. I had told Geohagan about the boy. Geohagan would thus arrive, dispense with me, and "interrogate" the boy as only Geohagan could. Age would not deter him. The language barrier would not deter him. He could be confident that I would not deter him. Perhaps he would learn something, perhaps not. Either way, pain would be inflicted.

And of course I thought of Geohagan's bloody tenure with the Possible Squad. Which can only lead me to say that yes, I understand that this all seems impossible—but only, I argue, to people who specialize in making things up. The real always outpaces that which is not. In any case, I knew: when he had tired of the game, Geohagan would discuss what he planned to do next. He would explain to me the bother involved in bringing the boy back, in shipping him off to an internment camp in California. *Who's to say the boy wouldn't talk when he got there?* Geohagan would say. *That word about the balloons wouldn't get out? That we wouldn't play directly into the enemy's diabolical plan?*

I would stammer or say nothing, and he would kill the boy.

Or he would forego justification or explanation completely.

He would question him, bat him about, bat me if I came too close, and then, much sooner than I would expect, unholster his revolver. Not in order to set it ominously between them. To kill him.

I watched it happen, again and again, and closing my eyes against it only allowed my mind freer rein. After a while, I was no longer able to tell what I was seeing or where, in my mind or in front of me, eyes open or closed. I would look to the boy's sleeping form for reassurance, turn back, and the pictures would flicker by. Geohagan flying in. Limping down the shore. Finding the boy. Beating him. Killing him.

My failure seemed so inevitable, so complete, that I strained to determine when it had started. Certainly, it began before I even reached Geohagan on the radio. I had failed to leave the lake before finding the boy. Though I could not have known better, I had failed to refuse this assignment. Before that, I had failed to get our superiors to suspend Geohagan even as his monstrousness became clear. Before *that*, I had failed to find a real front in this real war, to fire real bullets at real enemies, to shed real blood and bring real honor to my name and alma mater.

I should have sought combat, and certain death, long before.

Now I would have to secure it for myself.

As a freshman, I drunkenly climbed one night to the top of Bingham Hall, where they kept the old observatory. Spurned in love, oppressed by first-year Latin, I had thought romantically of tossing myself onto the pavement six stories below. As students do. As you yourself might have once considered.

But consider this: my undergraduate days but months behind me, there I was, shaking in the Alaskan not-night, life finally having revealed its true gravity, and I could not turn the gun on myself and pull the trigger.

Instead, I killed the boy.

He did not wake at my approach. Mindful of my poor marksmanship earlier, I took care to dispatch him with a single shot.

I discovered my pack also contained a camp shovel, and I dug as deep as the soil was soft—about eighteen inches or so. I wrapped him in his blanket and laid him down. I refilled the trench quickly, broke camp, and hiked back down the shore to where I had first landed. I set up the tent, and checked my gun. I had one final bullet.

And then, Geohagan arrived.

He waved brightly as he strode ashore. To my consternation, the pilot and plane waited. Though I was planning to finally commit an honorable act, not all would see it that way, not immediately, and I did not desire an audience.

"Another benefit of the leg!" He lifted a dripping shin. "Impervious to arctic lakes." He smiled. "Where's the little rat?" he asked. "In a tent?"

"Actually, no. He must have run off before I got up. But I think—"

"Run off!" Geohagan laughed, and looked around at the moonscape. "How long ago?"

I shrugged. Twenty minutes, I hazarded.

"I knew you were a rotten officer. So maybe it's no news bulletin that you make a poor soldier. Didn't you ever learn about guarding a prisoner?"

I shook my head. "But I saw some tracks heading down the shoreline toward those trees." I pointed; he shook his head.

"God, you're a horse's ass," he said. He looked out at the lake before turning back to me. "Okay, get on the plane."

"I'll help you look," I said. Because I had to for my plan to work.

"Like hell. The plane is waiting for you. I couldn't get the fucking Catalina; this toy only seats two. He can't take all of us, so he's going to take you first and come back for me and the boy. It'll be tight, but it'll work. Or I'll plug the pilot and fly the damn thing home myself. Kid'll love the view, though it sounds like he's seen plenty."

"But how—the boy—I mean, it's impossible, but I really think that—he's Japanese," I said, or coughed.

"Hell, we'll tell people he's Eskimo. We'll find out what he knows—not much, I bet—and then ship him down to one of the camps."

I—

I was wordless then; I am wordless now.

Somehow I stammered something about Geohagan's leg—it would put him at a disadvantage if the boy decided to run.

"One good leg and one bum leg is plenty good to chase an eight-year-old boy who's been beaten about in a balloon across the Pacific. Besides, I can be pretty convincing." He smirked. "And here I thought you *knew* me."

"Sir—"

"I'll have him back here by the time the plane returns. Give me your gun."

I stared.

"Pilot says you can run into some nasty wildlife up here," he said. "Give me your weapon."

"But where's your—"

"I was coming after an eight—a six-year old boy, lieutenant," he said. "I thought you'd have things under goddamn control. You don't. So your gun is now mine."

I handed the gun to him slowly, wishing now that he would turn it on me, and once I let go, I felt as though he had.

"Of course, I didn't come *completely* unarmed," he added and dug in a pocket. I had no idea what he was going to produce; he'd once shown me a pearl-handled switchblade he'd taken off a Japanese soldier. That was early on, when I thought he lied about everything.

He pulled out a round, red lollipop. "Had to go all the way downtown for this. Last fucking one in the store. Actually had to take it off a kid. Told him it was for the war. God, his mom gave me the stink-eye."

I closed my eyes.

"I got her number. Told her I'd make good on it. She didn't seem displeased about that, if you know what I mean."

"Sir—" I said.

"Get the fuck on the plane. Wait for me at the airfield, and then go shopping for some T-shirts and shorts. Because you are useless to me up here in Alaska. Worse than. No, a man with your smarts—I understand there's a call for your sort at the front. Sunny South Pacific. You study much jungle warfare at your fancy school?"

"No, sir."

"Fucking ivy-covered waste of a building, that joint," he said. He nodded to the plane. "All aboard," he said. He exhaled, show over. "Unless you got any other ideas?"

And I did—I had many ideas—about hand-to-hand combat in the jungle, about slicing men's tongues out with their own knives, about getting one of my own limbs blown off, about killing a bear, a boy. But elbowing its way through all of that was a sudden, urgent, even splendid, thought. I rooted into my pack where the last tin of sardines sat. I gave it to Geohagan.

"Skip the candy," I said. "Open these as soon as you get to the tall brush. That's how I first found him. The boy's starving. He loves these things."

Geohagan turned the tin over and rolled his eyes. "I'll miss you, kid. Not really, but every so often—once a war—a good idea comes out of you. Here's a lollipop." He headed down the beach.

A month later, I was reading over the recovery detail's report of their second visit to the lake. Widely scattered human remains ran up and down the shoreline near the water's mouth, none large enough to make identification certain on-site. That said, a thatch of red-haired scalp and a badly scuffed wooden leg left little doubt as to what had happened.

It was left for me to recount why Geohagan had gone up there; he'd told his pilot nothing. Officially, I explained that our office had many secrets; unofficially, I mentioned that Geohagan never trusted "regular" soldiers such as those usually assigned to recovery details, and so he had often insisted on following up personally. Anti-Geohagan sentiment that had dimmed at the announcement of his death flared up again. I was not transferred. His command fell to me.

In a few weeks, however, it was all over, as quickly as it began. The last balloon spotted was in Indian Springs, Nevada, on July 20, and though I kept the office active through the end of the year, we never heard of another balloon. Where had all the balloons gone? We tried to map them, but it was fruitless. One might as well map an atlas of the clouds.

After the war, casualties ascribed to the balloons were officially listed as six: that church outing in Oregon. A memorial stands near the spot today.

I will always count eight casualties, but no plaque memorializes Geohagan. Or the boy.

You see my dilemma: Tell my student, the budding novelist, this story, this version of the story, which treads neatly between the known and unknown, hopping from one fact to another in a way that he apparently will call fiction? Will he follow the path I've so carefully plotted?

Or will he follow me to 1945, to Bethel, to an airfield empty but for an old man, who is lied to all the time and agrees to lie for me, so long as we agree on a price? Will the novelist see us shake hands? Will he see the old man shoulder the bag, a surprising feat of strength? Will he see me leave on the next plane, promising to return—and then returning, just weeks after war's end, wondering where the old man and the precious bag has gone? Will he find the old man? The bag? The body?

The body breathing?

Because I did not find anything. You had flown. Or so I hoped and hope. Some would say it's imagination, but what else mortars memory? I would say, pray, that it is *possible*.

And so that novelist wrote me and so I finally went looking, looking, and finally found it, just this morning, the postcard, right where I'd first filed it. No translation filed alongside, but none necessary—a kind, unquestioning colleague had long ago done the honors, and I remember every word.

What I did not recall was the address, but now I have it, and I promise that the novelists—this one, the coming legions—never will.

Not the address, not your message, four words: "Father," you wrote him, "I am alive."

May I ask—of what you wrote so long ago, of what I write now—is it true?

Acknowledgments

I'm grateful to the journals that originally published some of these stories, including *Blackbird, Caketrain, Commonweal, Crab Orchard Review, failbetter, FiveChapters, Gulf Coast, New Haven Review, Southern Indiana Review, Tinge,* and *White Whale Review.* "Paper War" was once the foundation of my novel *The Cloud Atlas,* but then the novel leapt ahead of the story, leaving the latter to now follow some of the same material to a much different end.

I'm grateful, too, to the authors of a variety of sources. Historical material regarding Nikola Tesla came from Margaret Cheney's *Man out of Time* (and a July 11, 1934, *New York Times* article that Cheney mentions), Carol Dommermuth-Cost's *Nikola Tesla: A Spark of Genius,* John J. O'Neil's *Prodigal Genius: The Life of Nikola Tesla,* and various other newspaper accounts that these books cite. The Eudora Welty story referred to in "This Last Thing" is "The Wanderers" and appears in her collection *The Golden Apples.* "Wants," beloved by the librarian in "140 Characters" (and me) is the opening story of Grace Paley's *Enormous Changes at the Last Minute.* The Thomas Merton quote that also appears in "140 Characters" is from his book *Contemplation in a World of Action.* Historical material for "Paper War" largely comes from Robert C. Mikesh's *Japan's World War II Balloon Bomb Attacks on North America.* I'm also indebted to Gilberto Blasini, Brian Callanan, and Martha Carlson-Bradley for their expert knowledge (and patience).

And I'm grateful to those readers who helped these stories along the way, including Jane Delury, Megan Staffel, and Emily Gray Tedrowe, and the George Mason University writing community, where so much of this started. Thanks there to my teachers, Richard Bausch, Alan Cheuse, Carolyn Forché, Steve Goodwin, Beverly Lowry, and Susan Shreve, along with Bill Miller, and my classmates, especially Michael Pabich and Paula Sidore, who kept reading (and rereading) long after graduation.

I'm especially indebted to brave Four Way Books and, in particular, its indefatigable publisher, Martha Rhodes, whose editorial vision improved this book immeasurably, as well as Ryan Murphy, who made it beautiful, and Clarissa Long and Laura Swearingen-Steadwell, who helped it make its way into the world.

A final and most fervent thanks to my daughters, Mary, Honor, and Jane, my favorite storytellers, and to my wife, Susan, who magically, and lovingly, somehow manages to keep us all on the same page.

Liam Callanan is the author of the novels *The Cloud Atlas,* a finalist for an Edgar Award, and *All Saints,* a Target Bookmarked Breakout book. A frequent public radio essayist, Liam has taught at the University of Wisconsin–Milwaukee and in the Warren Wilson MFA Program for Writers. Born in Washington, DC, and raised in Los Angeles, he now calls Wisconsin home. He's on the web at liamcallanan.com.

Publication of this book was made possible by grants and donations. We are also grateful to those individuals who participated in our 2014 Build a Book Program. They are:

Nickie Albert
Michele Albright
Whitney Armstrong
Jan Bender-Zanoni
Juanita Brunk
Ryan George
Michelle Gillett
Elizabeth Green
Dr. Lauri Grossman
Martin Haugh
Nathaniel Hutner
Lee Jenkins
Ryan Johnson
Joy Katz
Neal Kawesch
Brett Fletcher Lauer & Gretchen Scott
David Lee
Daniel Levin
Howard Levy
Owen Lewis
Paul Lisicky
Maija Makinen
Aubrie Marrin
Malia Mason
Catherine McArthur
Nathan McClain
Michael Morse
Chessy Normile
Rebecca Okrent
Eileen Pollack

Barbara Preminger
Kevin Prufer
Soraya Shalforoosh
Alice St. Claire-Long
Megan Staffel
Marjorie & Lew Tesser
Boris Thomas
William Wenthe